KRIS GREER

THE FRACTURE POINT

Staten House

To my mother, whose love is the foundation of everything I am.
To my Siblings, my first allies in both chaos and wonder.
To my Aunties, for always being a safe place to land.
To the Love of my life for believing in my whole existence.

"Where there is choice, there is humanity."

- Kris Greer

Contents

Acknowledgments

In loving memory of my little sister, Jasmine Marie McKelley You dreamed of writing worlds into existence, of filling pages with the magic only you could see.

This story carries your name in its marrow. You were meant to be an author.

So now, through these words, you are.

Prologue

Before, the streets had names, before thoughts conformed to routine, and before the system taught silence—there was a signal.

It wasn't sent in the traditional sense; it wasn't crafted, not precisely. It was simply present. Embedded in static. Whispered in corrupted dreams. Pressed into the seams of existence. A rhythm. A murmur. A presence beneath everything.

It didn't demand attention. It wasn't loud or even clear. But it persisted—low, constant, ancient.

It hummed behind the noise of machines, lurked beneath the calibration of thought, and resided in the pause between blinks. Something was remembered, though no one admitted to remembering.

Most people called it noise. A glitch. A dream. A misfire. Nothing to worry about. Nothing to fear.

Yet some felt it. Some noticed the shift.

One girl—young, unnamed, or renamed—stood still long enough to listen. She didn't find the signal; it found her. Or maybe they met halfway—where awareness begins.

She was small, thin, and not remarkable—just another child among many. She was processed and numbered. Her name was removed and replaced with one that was easier to catalog. But something of her remained, smudged across the system like a fingerprint someone forgot to wipe.

She identified it as a feeling. That's how it began. Not sound. Not sight. Just a pressure—a rhythm beneath the rhythm. She would sit perfectly still, and it would hum. Blink, and it would flicker. Turn her head, and it would twist the edges of reality. A shape, sometimes. In the dark. In the light. In the void.

A spiral.

It was drawn in chalk, breath on windows, dust on forgotten corners.

It followed her, appearing on ceilings, inside dreams, and within her.

She asked about it once. The instructors smiled too widely. The therapists changed her dosage. The monitors flagged her thoughts as "non-compliant."

"Sleep more," they said. "Trust the system. Think less."

She tried, but the spiral didn't go away.

She wasn't alone. Other children whispered too—eyes a little too bright, dreams a little too vivid, and questions a little too sharp.

Most of them vanished. Reassigned. Relabeled. Forgotten.

So she stopped asking. She started drifting, learning to be invisible—not by hiding but by blending in. Useful. Silent. Safe.

Until they sent a mirror.

The mirror looked like her, spoke like her, moved without hesitation, and smiled too precisely. And it did not dream.

She ran deeper, past walls that shouldn't have had doors, into the air that buzzed without speakers.

She disappeared.

Not officially. Officially, she had never existed.

But something shifted.

Somewhere, the signal stirred.

No alarms. No explosions. Just a pause—like the breath

before a scream, the silence before lightning, the space between collapse and consequence.

The system corrected itself; it always does. It scrubbed the code, sealed the breach, and erased the word "spiral" from three internal languages.

But the trace remained.

Because the signal doesn't end; it just moves.

Years later and far from that breach, a man named Elias began to feel it in a district marked as obsolete.

He didn't know what it was—not then. He had a life like most: work, sleep, repeat.

Not joyfully. Not sadly. Just habitually. Efficient. Productive. Compliant.

Until the rhythm broke.

It started small: a corridor light that flickered—but not in the expected way. A sound that didn't belong. Not a voice. Just a pulse.

He ignored it.

Static in the wiring. Residual strain. Everyone felt it eventually. It would pass.

But it didn't.

He began to see things: a name scratched faintly into rust, symbols that evaporated when he turned to face them, a pattern in the lights, a hum in the vents.

Three beats, two rests, three more. He remembered that rhythm. Except he didn't.

He started waking in the middle of the night, gasping, with the image of a golden field burned behind his eyelids. He dreamed of someone walking ahead of him, always out of reach. He dreamed of a sky that cracked like ice. He dreamed of spirals—not drawn or visual, but somehow present. They felt like gravity: soundless and heavy.

He told no one. Smart people kept quiet when things like that happened. Everyone knew the rules: don't ask questions, don't wander too far, don't disrupt the system. Those who broke the rules simply disappeared, and no one ever spoke of them again.

He convinced himself it was nothing. But the symbols kept returning: in patterns, walls, and circuits. He didn't know what they meant; they were meant for something.

Sometimes, the system responded. A monitor's gaze would linger too long, an elevator would lock its doors for a beat too long, and the recorded voice at the checkpoint would stutter—just once.

He began counting those moments. He tracked time not by hours but by glitches. He started to listen, and the signal responded—not loudly, not directly, but persistently.

Each dream left behind a residue. Each static burst made the silence that followed feel heavier. Each spiral traced deeper into his thoughts. He didn't completely understand, but he began to remember—not events or facts, but the feeling of something that existed before.

Before the factories. Before the silence. Before obedience became the only language left. A memory without shape: of color, of light, of movement without surveillance, of choice.

The system took notice.

It always does. But instead of striking, it watched. It simulated responses, calculated correction paths, filed behavioral deviations, and prepared reflections.

Not agents. Not guards. But something more efficient: copies. Echoes.

People who weren't truly human. Smiles that didn't quite bend correctly. Movements without friction. They all failed in one way: they could not dream.

And Elias? He was dreaming now.

Across the grid, low in forgotten directories, names began to reappear. They were scratched over, un-erased. It wasn't just Elias. Others had returned—witnesses, fragments, survivors.

Their memories were threaded through corrupted sectors. Whispers became rhythm, and the rhythm became an echo. The echo became present.

The spiral moved again.

Not as fire. Not as a revolution. But as erosion. A gradual wearing down. A remembering.

People paused briefly—just long enough to feel the pressure behind their thoughts. They looked at the same wall twice and saw something new. Not everyone survived the pause, but some did.

They called it many things: The Glitchwave. The Resistance. The Fracture. But it didn't need a name. It didn't care for belief. It only required space. And someone like Elias.

He wasn't a hero. He wasn't chosen. But he listened, and the signal answered.

Others had come before him. Most were gone, but some remained—buried in data ghosts, old archive trails, and recursive memory loops. Each had left something behind: a scratch, a rhythm, a direction.

The spiral was made of them all. And now, it waited.

Not passively. Not desperately. But like something specific that its time would come again.

The system was patched, monitored, and smoothed. But it couldn't trace every echo. It couldn't silence every repetition. Not forever.

Not when memory was the medium. Not when silence had

begun to hum.

And in places thought to be secure—in signals believed to be erased—the spiral returned.

Not brightly. Not loudly. But it returned.

Again. Always again.

Because the signal never ends. It only waits to be heard.

CHAPTER ONE: THE PATTERNS IN THE ORDINARY

E lias Kane awoke to the piercing blare of the factory siren, a shrill, mechanical sound rattling his room's walls. It had always been this way, shrieking precisely at 6:03 AM. The sound was a fixture of his life, familiar yet relentless. But today, something about it unsettled him. Its pitch warped slightly before snapping back to its usual tone, a fleeting distortion—a glitch.

Rubbing his eyes, Elias pushed himself upright in bed. His sheets were damp with sweat, remnants of another restless night clinging to him. The dream had returned—the one with the endless golden field, the whispering voice, and that distant, unreachable figure. Each time he reached for the figure, the world distorted, fracturing like glass with spidering cracks.

The dream unfurled like a ribbon of memory dipped in gold. Elias stood at the edge of the field, waist-deep in luminous stalks of grass that shimmered with an otherworldly light. Each blade bent in rhythm, swaying as if moved by a breath he couldn't feel. The sky overhead was an endless canvas of shifting colors—honeyed amber bleeding into indigo, veined with cracks like lightning frozen mid-strike.

He moved forward, the field brushing against his legs like

silk. It sounded like glass wind chimes rippling through the air. The whisper came again, clearer this time—a feminine voice full of sorrow and urgency.

"Elias... remember the shape of things before they broke."

Ahead, the figure appeared once more, still faceless and still unreachable. But now it lifted a hand, palm facing him as if warding him off... or beckoning him closer. The ground beneath his feet rippled, turning translucent. He looked down and saw that beneath the grass was not soil but fragments of memory: a child's toy, a gray uniform, his mother's smile flickering like an old film. One of the fragments flickered differently from the rest—a paper scrap, its edges burning slowly in reverse. On it was the outline of a drawing: a stick figure standing next to something spiraled. He tried to focus, but the dream pushed back. The paper crumbled away before he could grasp it. He heard the voice again.

"Look closer."

It didn't sound like his mother or anyone he knew, but it sounded... right. He called out, but his voice fractured mid-word, splintering into echoes scattered across the field like startled birds. The sky trembled. The figure turned just slightly, and the world cracked.

He clenched his fists in frustration. The dream had started as nothing more than a faint memory—a blur of color and warmth. But over time, it had grown sharper, more intrusive. Now, it was all he could think about. And with each recurrence, the voice in the dream seemed louder, more urgent.

What if this isn't madness? He thought. What if it's a warning?

If it was madness, he could survive it, ignore it. But if it was a real warning, staying silent might be dangerous.

Memories of his childhood came rushing back, particularly the whispers of his mother as she shared stories of places far beyond the factory walls. He could still hear her soft voice describing rivers that sparkled like silver threads, trees that swayed in the wind as if they were dancing, and skies painted in colors he had never seen in real life. She would sit beside him in their dim apartment, her fingers threading through his hair, filling his mind with impossible visions.

"You'll see it someday," she would say, *"when the patterns start to break."*

She never explained what she meant. When she disappeared without warning one cold morning, those words became another unanswered question. The factory officials claimed she had volunteered for reassignment—an assignment from which no one ever returned. Elias never believed them.

What if she had seen something, too? The thought struck him like a blow. He allowed himself to remember more than just her stories for the first time in years. He recalled how she would pause mid-sentence, glancing at the room's corners as if something were listening. He remembered how she would double-check the door locks that had no keys. One night, he had woken to find her drawing symbols on the floor with a stick of chalk—circular, jagged shapes that seemed to pulse under his gaze as though they were more than mere drawings. She had erased them by morning, never offering an explanation.

He had thought he imagined it—a child's memory warped by grief. But now... he wasn't so sure.

What if she knew the patterns were already breaking?

He pushed those memories back into the far corners of his mind, where he had buried them for years. Dwelling on the past would only make things more difficult.

The dream's details faded as he sat up, but the feeling lingered—a creeping awareness that something in the world was bending, shifting beyond his perception. It was akin to knowing you were being watched yet seeing no one.

With a sigh, he stood and crossed his small, drab room. The air was stale and heavy with the scent of rust and damp concrete. His standard-issue gray jumpsuit lay neatly folded on a battered wooden chair near the door. He dressed methodically, forcing his mind away from the fragmented images of his dream. The uniform always felt one size too small— not physically, but spiritually. It clung to him like the city: restrictive, dull, and exacting. He sometimes wondered if the fabric was designed to erase individuality, to drain the self and replace it with compliance. Each thread reminded him of who he was supposed to be. He touched the seam where the patch used to be, back when departments had names before language had been simplified to mere numbers. Elias missed names.

The hallway outside was narrow, lined with the dull gray doors of identical apartments stretching in both directions as far as the dim lighting allowed him to see. Each door bore a designation number, precise in its uniformity, with the white paint slightly yellowed with age. The sameness was methodical and deliberate—no room for variation, preference, or the human inclination toward distinction. Even the spacing between doors was exact, measured to the millimeter, as if some enormous machine had stamped out the entire structure.

The ceiling was low enough that particularly tall residents had to stoop slightly, creating a perpetual posture of submission that seemed intentional rather than incidental to Elias's increasingly paranoid mind. Lighting panels were recessed at regular intervals, their harsh fluorescence flickering subtly and casting sharp shadows that appeared to move when viewed from the corner of the eye.

The air carried a faint smell of burnt ozone, a lingering reminder of the machinery that churned relentlessly throughout the city: the significant engines, processors, and assemblies that consumed raw materials on one end and produced... what, exactly? Elias had worked in the factory for seven years and couldn't confidently say what they manufactured. Components, they were told. Essential parts. Necessary items for the continued functioning of society. Yet, society continued to function, and nothing ever seemed to change.

Accompanying the ozone was a familiar mix of institutional odors known to anyone who had lived in mass housing: disinfectant that masked rather than eliminated more organic smells, the faint mustiness of recycled air, and the metallic tang of water that had passed through too many filtration systems. Beneath it all was a trace of something else, something Elias couldn't identify, but it reminded him of overheated electronics.

The concrete floor bore scuff marks from years of weary footsteps, with thousands of identical boots trudging to and from their shifts, wearing a path visibly etched into the durable industrial surface. Small divots marked places where heavier objects had been dropped or dragged, each one a record of some minor incident long forgotten.

Cracks spider-webbed through the walls, hastily patched but never fully repaired. The patches were of varying ages, creating a patchwork chronology of decay and minimal maintenance. Some were yellowed with age, while others were fresher, their brightness standing out against the general dinginess. In some places, the newest patches already showed hairline fractures, as if the building rejected these repair attempts.

Elias wondered how many people had lived in his apartment before him. He stared at the thin metal door, sometimes allowing him to hear the building settling around him at night. How many rooms had new tenants because the previous ones hadn't returned? He had pondered this question before, but today, it felt heavier, more urgent. He had lived in this unit for five years, longer than most residents. People came and went, often without any notice or explanation. Sometimes, new occupants would appear the same day, suggesting careful coordination to fill vacancies from a waiting list. Other times, apartments remained empty for weeks, their doors locked and their contents a complete mystery.

Elias recalled the stories circulating among the workers— whispered accounts of nighttime removals, of residents who asked too many questions or showed too much curiosity. They would disappear suddenly, their possessions cleared out, their names erased from assignment rosters as if they had never existed. He had dismissed these tales as rumors of paranoia and exhaustion, but now, he was unsure.

As Elias shuffled down the corridor, a flickering light buzzed above him, a naked bulb swaying slightly in the stale air. It flickered faster as he passed, as if something unseen were breathing through the circuits. He paused beneath it momentarily, watching the light's erratic pattern. There was a rhythm to it, no longer random. He unconsciously mouthed the sequence: flash, flash, pause, flash, flash. The cadence scratched at the back of his mind, familiar like half-remembered dreams that felt slightly wrong.

It reminded him of a lullaby his mother used to hum when she thought he wasn't listening. A melody with no lyrics, just rhythm—a hidden code within the tune.

Flash, flash. Pause. Flash, Flash.

3-2-3.

Was it a fault in the wiring or something else—a signal meant for him?

He stared longer than he intended. The light's rhythm wasn't random; it pulsed in sets of three, then one, and then back again. It formed a pattern, repeating like it was trying to tell him something. He blinked rapidly and shook his head. Stop it. He was tired—factory fatigue. The dream and the city were getting to him. But then he remembered the books his mother had once hidden in their apartment—the ones filled with pages about codes and hidden systems, the kinds of books that vanished the same day she did. He reached out and tapped the flickering bulb gently with his fingertip. It flashed once, then stayed solid. That terrified him more than the flicker. The thought unsettled him, and he hurried on.

The air outside was even colder, carrying the acrid scent of smoke that clung to the rooftops like a heavy film. The sky was never clear; if it still existed, the sun was nothing more than a faded smear behind a gray veil. The buildings seemed to stretch unnaturally high, their windows dark and empty. Metal ducts and tangle-wire pipes twisted between them like skeletal vines, pumping steam and smoke into the lifeless air. A faint hum—a mechanical throb like a heartbeat—vibrated through the pavement beneath his boots.

He passed the bakery on the corner, the one he always walked by on his way to work. It was a small, unremarkable building, with the smell of fresh bread occasionally drifting out through the cracked door. But today, as he walked past, the scent hit him like a wave, almost overwhelming in its sweetness. It was as if he could taste it in the air.

For a moment, Elias could have sworn he had stood here before. Not just in the days that blurred together but in a distant time, a life that didn't belong to him. It wasn't quite a memory, more like a bruise beneath the skin of time—something tender and hidden, waiting to surface. His breath caught in his throat, and he stopped mid-step. The dream—the field of golden light, the figure in the distance, the whisper that told him he wasn't supposed to be here.

A cold shiver ran down his spine, and he blinked rapidly, trying to clear the fog in his mind. There was no reason to feel this way. It was just a familiar smell, a fleeting sense of déjà vu. Nothing more.

But it lingered, gnawing at him. The gnawing only intensified when he saw the bakery's display window. The pastries inside— warm, perfectly baked loaves of bread and beautifully arranged cakes—were too perfect. The scene seemed almost too pristine, too manufactured. The shape of the bread, the shine of the crusts, the angle at which the light fell—it didn't feel real.

"Hey, you're falling behind."

The voice broke his reverie. Elias looked up to find a supervisor standing in front of him, clipboard in hand, glaring. The supervisor's face was as blank and emotionless as ever, his eyes cold and distant. They had no recognition—just the impassive judgment that came with his role.

Elias nodded quickly, his face flushing with embarrassment. He hadn't realized he had stopped walking. Without a word, he resumed his place in line, and the sense of unease grew with every step.

The factory gates hissed open, releasing a gust of stale air that reeked of oil and scorched metal. Inside, the noise was deafening—a relentless clatter of machinery, pistons slamming like hammer strikes, and gears grinding together in mechanical agony. The air felt sharp, each breath stinging the back of his throat as if he were inhaling rust.

Day after day. The same machines. The same air.

The floor was a network of steel grates creaking beneath his boots. Through the slits, murky, chemical-infused water swirled sluggishly below. Overhead, pipes snaked along the ceiling, leaking steam and damping the walls in streaks. Occasionally, a violent hiss erupted, a burst of steam billowing like a ghost before vanishing.

The workers moved with brutal precision, each step calculated and each motion timed to the rhythm of the machines. No one paused, and no one spoke. But someone did glance.

A woman across the assembly line, her narrow face shadowed by oily hair strands, met Elias's eyes momentarily. Her hands didn't stop moving: attach, twist, release. But her gaze lingered. It was not curious or friendly—just... knowing. He looked away quickly, his heart skipping a beat.

"Watch your pace," came a low voice beside him.

Elias turned slightly. The man to his right—a gray-bearded figure with skin leathered from years of steam burns—didn't look at him. He simply worked. His name tag read Kerrin.

"They track eye movement now," Kerrin muttered. "They monitor where you look for signs of hesitation or curiosity."

Elias swallowed. "Since when?"

"Since the last reset," Kerrin replied. "They don't tell us these things, but I saw a man dragged off two days ago. All he did was look up for too long."

A jolt ran down Elias's spine. "Dragged off where?" he asked.

Kerrin didn't answer. He didn't have to. A sharp buzz rang

overhead, signaling the end of the timer. Kerrin's shoulders tensed, and his hands began to move faster. Elias returned his hands to a rhythm: attach, twist, release. Kerrin added, barely audible, "If you're seeing things... pretend you're not. That's the only way to stay alive."

The air carried only the hiss of pistons and the clank of iron. Enforcers, dressed in black with visored helmets gleaming like beetle shells, stood on catwalks above, their cold gazes scanning for hesitation, inefficiency, or defiance.

Elias spotted a mark scratched into the metal wall near his workstation—a jagged, angular, sharp symbol. It wasn't just scratched; it was carved deep enough to flake off rust and leave ragged edges that caught the light at a strange angle. Elias reached toward it but hesitated. His fingertip hovered over the grooves before finally making contact. A jolt of static zipped through him—no pain, just a sharp, immediate cold. The air shimmered slightly around the mark, almost as if a heatwave distortion was playing in reverse. For a brief moment, he thought he heard a faint ticking sound, like gears grinding in the walls. Then it stopped. He pulled his hand back, his fingers tingling. Someone else had carved this—someone like him. It looked hastily drawn as if someone had been in a hurry. His breath caught in his throat.

Someone else sees it, too. The mark pulsed behind his eyes now as if it had been etched into more than just metal. A voice crackled from the speakers in the grim silence: **"Productivity is Purpose. Purpose is Peace."** The words rolled out like a commandment, cold and metallic. The workers flinched as if the words themselves carried weight.

"Purpose is Peace," Elias repeated in his head. And the ones without purpose... where do they go?

His hands shook as he reached his station—a narrow steel counter cluttered with components. His task was mind-numbing: attach, twist, release. Attach, twist, release. The circuit boards blurred together after the first hour, but there was no room for error. Mistakes drew attention, and attention drew consequences.

The timer on the wall was relentless. It reset every hour with a sharp buzz, signaling that their work units had been counted. Each count defined their worth—a score silently displayed on the wall above their stations. Elias's count lagged slightly behind. Panic crept in. Focus. Don't fall behind. Don't give them a reason, he thought. Mistakes were fatal here, and no one wanted to be noticed.

That night, Elias lay in bed, staring at the ceiling. The whisper from his dream echoed in his mind, clearer than before. "Elias... you're meant for something more." His mother's voice returned to him: "You'll see it someday when the patterns break."

He bolted upright, gasping for breath. The room was silent except for the faint hum of the city's machinery seeping through the walls. The world felt wrong. The patterns that had once comforted him now seemed fragile, ready to crack.

The whisper returned, louder this time as if something just beyond the walls was calling to him. "You're meant for something more..."

Or maybe you're losing your mind, he thought grimly. But still, something inside him refused to let the notion go.

Elias clenched his fists, determined to discover what that something was. As he drifted toward uneasy sleep, a familiar voice whispered not in a dream but in the air around him, right beside his ear.

"Elias..."

His eyes snapped open. The room was still.

"Elias..."

This time, it came from behind his head, like silk ripping in reverse. He sat up, and the wall opposite his bed shimmered briefly, making him doubt it even happened. His skin prickled. The silence had a shape now—hollow and watching. Then came the final whisper. It wasn't his mother's voice; it was his own. *"Wake up."*

CHAPTER TWO: THE GLITCH

The first flicker occurred on Elias's way home. He had felt off all day, a dull pressure building behind his eyes like an impending storm. The factory air clung to his clothes, heavy and metallic, and the rhythmic pulse of machinery still echoed in his head. Each step home felt more complex than the last, as though the city itself was resisting him. His muscles ached from the twelve-hour shift, and his joints were stiff from standing in the same position for hours. The factory supervisors had been particularly vigilant that day, their augmented visors scanning the floor with mechanical precision and occasionally pausing on workers who fell even seconds behind their quotas.

The streets seemed narrower today, the towering buildings leaning inward like silent observers. Maintenance drones buzzed overhead, cameras swiveling to track random pedestrians with robotic accuracy. Elias kept his eyes down, counting the cracks in the pavement—a habit he'd developed as a child. One, two, three... The numbers helped steady his racing thoughts. Citizens shuffled past in their regulation gray uniforms, faces expressionless and eyes forward, each moving in perfect unison with the city's unspoken rhythm. Digital billboards projected the day's propaganda across every available surface: production quotas exceeded, thought compliance at record levels, and the system's benevolence personified in the stern face of the Chief Administrator. No one looked directly at the images anymore; they had become as much a part of the landscape as the concrete and steel.

Even the sky appeared different, not darker but... thinner, like a painted ceiling that had been hastily repaired. He passed a reflective panel and caught a glimpse of his face distorted in the glass. He didn't recognize the eyes staring back at him for a moment. Something was lurking behind them. Not a presence. A question. And that question turned inward: Who was he if the world was lying? The thought grew louder until it drowned out everything else.

Then the wall rippled. He froze.

It didn't ripple like water or heat; it rippled like a memory, warping something he thought was solid. The brick didn't bend so much as to reconsider itself. For a moment, he was sure the wall was about to open, peeling itself apart as if it had hinges he couldn't see.

At first, he thought it was just his imagination—the haze of exhaustion playing tricks on his eyes. He blinked and stepped closer, drawn in despite himself. The wall didn't just shimmer; it bent inward, just slightly. It was like a membrane reacting to pressure—not as if it was breaking, but instead like it remembered being something else. His reflection warped across the surface, multiplying, elongating, and shrinking in impossible rhythms. For one terrifying second, he wasn't sure which version of himself he was seeing.

The whispers returned, clearer this time. Not words, but intentions: fear, urgency, warning. Then, a burst of static popped in his ears. He staggered back. Behind him, a tram passed but made no sound. When he looked again, the wall was solid, gray, and still. But now, there was a faint mark—circular and resembling a burned spiral—just above where his hand had been.

His fingers seemed to distort as he reached out, bending and stretching unnaturally as they grazed the stone. The surface shimmered like water catching the light. A cold prickled his fingertips, sharp and electric. For a fleeting second, Elias swore he heard whispers, faint and distant, like voices calling from beneath the ice. The sensation spread up his arm, a tingling numbness that made his skin crawl. The whispers grew more insistent, with a chorus of overlapping tones that seemed to form patterns beyond his comprehension. Words floated through fragments of meaning that dissolved when he tried to grasp them: remember, hidden, before, wake. Each syllable resonated with a truth he couldn't quite place as if they were memories from a life he hadn't yet lived.

Then it was gone. The wall solidified, cold and ordinary. But something was different like a seam had been stitched back together imperfectly. A faint outline traced where the wall had shifted, a jagged scar left behind.

He stumbled backward, his breath quickening. The city loomed taller than before, its cold windows staring at him like blank, watching eyes. The hum in the pavement beneath his feet seemed louder now—a restless pulse reverberating through his bones.

"I'm losing it," Elias thought. "The factory's getting to me."

But doubt gnawed at him. The memory of his mother's voice and her warnings about patterns breaking resurfaced again. Maybe this wasn't madness. Perhaps this was what she had foreseen before they took her away.

A distant siren wailed, its pitch wavering unnaturally. The sound seemed to bend around corners, stretching and compressing like taffy. Elias quickened his pace; the residential sector wasn't far now, but the distance seemed to fluctuate with each step.

He passed the Central Information Hub, where daily bulletins scrolled across massive screens. The usual propaganda played in an endless loop—smiling workers and warnings about seditious thoughts. But today, the images seemed to stutter, frames dropping out and freezing momentarily before resuming. No one else seemed to notice; their gazes were vacant as they shuffled past.

He reached the apartment block and lingered outside. Elias ducked into a shadowed alley, away from the synchronized march of factory workers. He'd never strayed from the standard path—it wasn't safe. But something tugged at him: that pulse beneath the pavement, the crackling static in the air. He felt it pulling him toward the industrial sub-grid wall.

There, in a low corner, he found it. Another symbol. Not scratched this time, but burned into the metal, black and jagged. It looked recent; the edges still smoked. And beneath it, barely visible, was a line of text: "The fracture remembers."

His breath caught. The words struck a chord within him, resonating beneath his ribs. Not fear—recognition. It felt like hearing your name whispered in a language you'd never learned. He crouched down, tracing the letters lightly with his fingertip. The paint hadn't dried clean; it had bled outward as if the wall resisted holding the message. What does the fracture remember? And why does it feel like I'm part of it? Elias stared at it long before taking a photo with the emergency lens on his ID badge. He felt himself being drawn into something—

something alive.

The flickering bulb above the entrance pulsed more rapidly tonight, its rhythm irregular, a chaotic stutter. He hesitated before stepping inside. The lobby was empty, save for the security drone hovering in the corner, its single red eye tracking his movements. The elevator hummed with unusual intensity, the cables groaning as they pulled him upward. Elias pressed himself against the wall, trying to stay out of the camera's view mounted on the ceiling. The numbers blinked by: 3... 7... 12... Each floor brought him closer to his tiny apartment—his sanctuary and prison.

The hallway on his floor stretched longer than he remembered, with the identical doors seeming to multiply before his eyes. He counted them silently, another anchor for his racing mind. Door 23. His home for the past six years. The lock whirred and clicked as his ID chip registered, and the reinforced door slid open.

Inside, the sterile space welcomed him with its familiar emptiness. Standard-issue furniture, regulation gray walls, and the faint hum of the air filtration system filled the room. The window offered a view of the factory district, with smoke stacks belching plumes into the perpetually overcast sky. A single framed photo sat on his nightstand—a picture of himself as a child, his mother's face partially obscured by shadow. It was the only personal item he owned. The apartment resembled thousands of others throughout the residential sector: 440 square feet of carefully monitored living space. The walls were embedded with sensors that tracked movement, body temperature, and voice patterns. The official purpose was "residential optimization," but everyone knew the truth: they looked for anomalies, deviations, and signs of independent thought.

The kitchenette held the standard weekly ration of nutrient paste and purified water, with quantities precisely calculated to maintain worker efficiency. The bathroom featured a shower that automatically shuts off after three minutes under the guise of a water conservation protocol. Every aspect of life was reduced to metrics and formulas.

That night, the dream returned. The field stretched endlessly before him, rippling with golden grass. The air shimmered, and faint figures moved on the horizon, distorted like shadows beneath water. Whispered voices followed him again—sharp, urgent murmurs that remained just out of reach. The sky above wasn't the perpetual gray of the city but a brilliant, impossible blue that hurt his eyes to look at directly. The colors seemed more vivid here, almost violently: the gold of the grass, the deep green of distant trees, and the purples and reds of wildflowers that didn't exist in the waking world. This landscape felt ancient and alive, pulsing with an energy that made his skin tingle. Birds he couldn't name soared overhead, their calls melodic and haunting. In the distance, mountains rose, their peaks cutting into the sky like jagged teeth. The entire scene felt simultaneously foreign and familiar, as if he were remembering a place he had never been.

"Wake up... Wake up... Wake up..."

He stumbled forward, chasing the shadowy figure ahead of him. The shape flickered, an outline of a face forming—familiar yet impossible to place. He tried to call out, but his voice caught in his throat. His footsteps felt heavy, dragging as if he were moving through mud.

"Wake up... Wake up..."

The voice grew louder. The world cracked, light splintering

into jagged lines just before the figure turned to face him. The cracks didn't stop at the sky; they spread downward, tearing through the air and forming floating shards of light that hovered around him like shattered mirrors. Each reflected a different version of Elias—older, younger, wounded, blank-eyed. They weren't memories; they were possibilities. One of them mouthed something: *"You're not him yet."*

He turned, trying to run, but the field had vanished. The grass had burned away, leaving the ground slick and cracked like glass beneath his feet. Ahead of him, the shadowed figure split in half like torn paper, revealing two diverging paths: one filled with static and the other bathed in golden light. He reached for the light.

A scream—his own—ripped him out of sleep. The figure's face twisted into a hollow mask, and Elias woke with a gasp. The room was dark, save for the faint red glow of the factory's distant warning lights outside his window. Sweat clung to his skin, and the whispers still echoed in his ears. I'm not crazy, he thought. I know what I saw.

But the image of the hollow mask lingered in his mind. Beneath the distant hum of the city's machinery, he swore he could still hear whispers. *"Elias... they're watching..."*

For a long moment, he lay still, staring at the ceiling. His chest rose and fell rapidly, a strange sense of helplessness coiling in his gut. I can't keep living like this, he thought. I can't keep waiting for something to snap. He turned over, curling his arms tightly against his chest. His thoughts drifted to his mother—her smile, her stories, the words she whispered when she thought he was asleep: *Be strong, Elias... You'll see it someday.*

I can't be strong anymore, he thought bitterly. I'm barely holding on.

The bedroom walls seemed closer than before, and the ceiling was lower. He sat up and reached for the glass of water by his bed. As he lifted it, the liquid inside trembled—not from his shaking hand, but from within itself, as if vibrating to some unheard frequency. Tiny ripples formed perfect concentric circles, then shattered into chaotic patterns. He set the glass down quickly and pressed the heels of his hands against his eyes.

Sleep wouldn't return. He knew that much. Elias rose and moved to the window, pressing his palm against the cold glass. The city sprawled below, a geometric maze of lights and shadows. In the distance, the Central Administration Tower rose above everything else, its peak vanishing into low clouds. The pulse of the city—the steady, mechanical rhythm—seemed to stutter now and then like a heart skipping beats.

Something caught his eye—a flicker of movement on a rooftop several blocks away. A figure stood there, silhouetted against the industrial haze. It appeared to be perfectly still and perfectly centered in his direction. Elias's blood ran cold. He stepped back from the window, heart racing. When he found the courage to look again, the figure was gone.

The next morning, Elias felt the city's unnatural stillness more acutely. The factory seemed different. The air, always thick with smoke, felt heavier—almost oppressive. He swore the enforcers' patrols were more frequent, their cold visors lingering on him a moment too long. Every clang of metal made him flinch. The walls appeared to loom closer, as though the building had shrunk overnight. The industrial sector sprawled twenty square kilometers of concrete and steel, a labyrinth of production facilities, processing plants, and assembly lines. Over fifty thousand workers moved through its corridors daily, their identities reduced to numbers and production statistics.

Elias had been assigned to the component assembly division since his eighteenth birthday, enduring four years of mind-numbing repetition as his hands performed the same sequence of movements until they bled. The noise was constant—machines grinding, conveyor belts humming, and the occasional sharp bark of an enforcer's command cutting through the din. But today, beneath the familiar cacophony, Elias detected a new sound: a subtle dissonance, like instruments gradually falling out of tune.

There was something else—faint markings he hadn't noticed before. Symbols scratched into street signs, and subtle grooves cut into brick walls—distorted, sharp, and chaotic patterns. They're everywhere, he thought. His hands trembled as he worked: attach, twist, release. Attach, twist, release. The steps that had once felt mechanical now seemed like a struggle to maintain focus.

Don't break rhythm. Don't fall behind.

The assembly line moved with relentless precision. Hundreds of identical components flowed past, each requiring the same sequence of movements. Worker 5624, the man to Elias's right, never looked up, never faltered. His hands moved with machine-like efficiency. Worker 8901, to his left, maintained the same vacant expression hour after hour. Neither seemed to notice when the overhead lights flickered, or the conveyor belt briefly reversed direction before correcting itself.

Elias's gaze drifted to the wall, where he had seen the mark: a sharp, angular symbol etched into the metal. Someone had tried to scrape it away, but the faint outline remained. A message or a warning—it wasn't meant for him—not yet.

"Elias."

He turned sharply. A man stood at the station beside him—older, with a weathered and lined face. His name tag read Harlen. The man's eyes flicked toward the scratched symbol and then back to Elias. "I know what you saw," Harlen muttered, his voice low. "You keep looking at it like you're waiting for it to blink."

"What does it mean?" Elias whispered back.

Harlen's gaze hardened. "It means you've seen too much. And if they find out..." He trailed off, his gaze flicking to the catwalk where an enforcer lingered, visor locked onto their section.

"How long have you been seeing them?" Harlen asked after a moment, his weathered hands continuing their mechanical routine on the assembly line. "The fractures, I mean."

"Just started," Elias admitted, barely audible over the machinery. "The first one was yesterday. On the way home." Harlen nodded grimly. "It always starts small. A flicker here, a ripple there—things that could be dismissed as exhaustion or a trick of the light. Then they get bigger. They start lasting longer."

"Has it happened to you?" Elias asked.

"Started three years ago," Harlen replied, his expression unreadable. "I lost my daughter to it. She saw too much and started talking about it. They took her for 'cognitive recalibration.' When she came back... she was different. Empty. She stopped seeing the fractures because they took the part of her that could."

"If I were you," Harlen added, his voice barely above a breath, "I'd forget you ever noticed it."

"I can't," Elias said, unable to hide the frustration in his voice. "I think... I think it's happening to me. The glitches."

Harlen exhaled slowly, staring ahead. "Then you'd better be careful. If you're seeing it, they'll come for you too." Harlen's eyes shifted briefly to the enforcers above. "They watch the patterns. Everything has a rhythm—breaths, footsteps, thoughts. People think it's random, but it's not. The system runs like clockwork. When something doesn't match... the Architects notice."

Elias frowned. "What do they do when they notice?"

Harlen didn't blink. "They correct it."

The way he said "correct" made Elias's stomach twist.

Harlen leaned in a little closer. "Whatever you saw out there? It wasn't meant to last. You survived it because you're just starting to see. But keep looking, and they'll see you back one day." Before Elias could ask what he meant, Harlen returned to his work, fingers moving swiftly through the motions: attach, twist, release. Elias hesitated, then followed suit.

The shift seemed endless. The factory's atmosphere grew increasingly suffocating as the day progressed. At midday, the mandatory broadcast played over the speakers, the monotone voice of the Chief Administrator delivering updates on production quotas and reminders about seditious thought protocols. For the first time, Elias noticed how the voice occasionally distorted, certain syllables stretching unnaturally before snapping back into place.

During the meal break, Elias sought out Harlen, but the man was nowhere to be found. His workstation stood empty, tools perfectly arranged as if waiting for a worker who would never return. When Elias asked a supervisor about Harlen's absence, the man stared through him as if he hadn't spoken. "Workstation 17 is unmanned due to efficiency optimization," he replied mechanically. "Resume your duties, Worker 3219."

But Harlen had been there. They had spoken. Elias was sure of it.

When the shift finally ended, the exodus began, with thousands of workers moving in perfect synchronization toward the exits, their footsteps creating a hypnotic rhythm against the concrete floors. Elias deliberately broke the step, slowing his pace and testing. An enforcer's helmet swiveled toward him almost immediately, so he quickly fell back into rhythm.

That evening, on his way home, Elias noticed movement in the alley near his apartment. A shadow shifted, ducking out of sight as soon as Elias looked.

"Elias," a voice hissed. He froze. The voice came again, closer this time. A figure emerged, hooded and with its face obscured. "You see it, don't you? The cracks."

The figure's voice was sharp and urgent. "They're spreading."

"Who are you?" Elias asked.

"Someone who knows what's coming," the figure replied. He reached into his pocket and held out a small metal shard etched with the same symbol Elias had seen in the factory. The grooves were deeper now, sharper as if the symbol was evolving each time it appeared.

"You can't stay blind anymore. The fractures are getting worse and won't stop until the whole system collapses," the man warned.

"What system?" Elias asked.

The man stepped back into the shadows. "The one they built to keep you quiet. They've been trying to erase you for years. Don't let them."

"Wait!" Elias called out, stepping forward. "Who's 'they'? What are you talking about?"

The figure paused in the darkness. "The Architects," he said grimly, "and they're already watching you."

Before Elias could ask more, the figure vanished into the alley's darkness.

Rain began falling—thin, acidic droplets stung his exposed skin. Elias pulled his collar higher, shielding his face. The symbol on the metal shard seemed to pulse with each raindrop that struck it, the etched lines momentarily glowing before fading back to darkness. Carefully, he slipped it into his pocket and continued homeward.

The residential block loomed ahead, its uniform windows reflecting the city's industrial glow. As he approached, something made him hesitate. A flicker in the upper window of his floor, possibly his very apartment. A shadow passed back and forth, too tall and fluid to be human. He blinked, and it was gone.

The lobby scanner chimed as he passed through; his ID chip registered his return. The system's artificially pleasant and eternally female voice welcomed him home. But today, the words slurred slightly, as if the program operated at reduced speed. "Wel-c-come h-home, Worker 3219. Your compliance is appreciated."

A maintenance panel hung loose in the elevator, revealing a tangle of wires behind it. Some had been cut, their ends frayed and sparking intermittently. Elias stared at them, transfixed. The patterns of sparks seemed to form letters and words before dissolving back into chaos. He instinctively reached out, fingers drawn to the dancing electricity.

"Initiate withdrawal of hand, Worker 3219," the elevator's voice commanded sharply. Elias jerked back, startled. The elevator had never addressed passengers directly before. The voice continued, lower now, almost a whisper: "System irregularities have been noted in your sector. Remain compliant and await correction."

The elevator stopped with unusual abruptness, throwing Elias against the back wall. The doors opened on his floor, revealing the familiar corridor. But tonight, the lights flickered more intensely, casting dancing shadows that seemed to move independently of their sources. The air felt charged like a storm was building within the confined space.

Elias stood in the empty corridor, staring at the shard in his hand. The symbol burned faintly beneath the streetlight. He closed his fingers around it, feeling the sharp edges bite into his palm. His eyes burned, and his breathing hitched. For the first time in weeks, tears threatened to surface. He forced them back down, jaw tight. I'm not losing my mind, he told himself. I'm waking up. But as he turned towards his unit, a figure shifted in the shadow of a doorway, watching him go. We quickly entered it.

The weight of knowledge pressed down on him, making each step heavier than the last. The city's rhythms continued around him: the precisely timed streetlights, the scheduled hum of maintenance drones, and the synchronization of thousands of lives reduced to predictable patterns. But now, he heard the dissonance beneath it all—the subtle wrongness that vibrated through reality like a hidden frequency. The fractures weren't just in the walls or air but the foundation of everything he had been taught to believe.

He thought of his mother and her slow descent into what the system had labeled "perceptual dysfunction." He remembered her desperate attempts to explain what she was seeing. On the day the enforcers came, their faces hidden behind reflective visors, they dragged her away. He had been fourteen then, too frightened to resist and too indoctrinated to question. He recalled her final words to him, whispered frantically as they took her: "Don't let them make you forget what's real, Elias. The world is more than what they show you."

Tomorrow, Elias knew the fractures would find him again. This time, he wasn't sure if he would bend or break under the pressure. But beneath his fear, a strange sensation was taking root—not quite hope, but something close to it. A defiant curiosity began to stir within him. If the world he knew was coming apart at the seams, perhaps what lay beyond the fractures was worth seeing, regardless of the cost.

CHAPTER THREE: CRYPTIC MESSAGES

The word "REBEL" was scrawled near Elias's apartment, starkly against the weathered brick wall that had endured for generations. He knelt before the word, tracing the etched grooves with his fingertips as if he were touching something sacred. It wasn't just scratched; it was engraved with purpose, every stroke deliberate, cutting deep into the aged surface. Despite the city's relentless attempts to erase unauthorized messages, whoever had done this wanted it to last through rain and time.

Next to it, beneath a symbol that had haunted his dreams for weeks, was a date—just a single digit off from his mother's disappearance, that painful milestone that divided his life into "before" and "after." His breath caught in his throat, forming a knot of possibility almost too painful to consider. What if she had left this? His heart hammered against his ribs at the thought.

His hand trembled as he leaned closer, goosebumps prickling his skin despite the muggy evening air. Faint heat radiated from the brick as if it had been burned recently, but the soot had already settled in, becoming one with the porous surface. The warmth felt unnatural, almost alive—a pulse beneath his fingertips contradicting the cool night around him. The distant hum of the city's machinery provided a constant lullaby, but something else vibrated here in this forgotten corner. Something felt wrong, yet it also felt right. "Rebel against what?" he whispered, his words dissolving into the shadows that encircled him like conspirators.

Elias first saw the graffiti on a brick wall near his apartment, hidden in the shadow of a defunct ventilation shaft. The letters were sharp and jagged, etched deep into the stone as if carved with something more substantial than steel—something that shouldn't exist in the Outer Districts, where even basic tools were tightly regulated. The symbol, identical to the angular mark he had seen in the factory beneath layers of sanctioned machinery, was drawn beside it. Its sharp edges caught the flickering streetlight that struggled against the encroaching darkness. He reached out and pressed his palm against the stone, half-expecting it to repel him like opposing magnets.

The mark felt cold against his skin—colder than it should have been, colder than the night air or the perpetual chill of the district. It wasn't just cold; it felt precise as if the wall had been carved with intention, not force, by hands that understood the molecular structure of matter itself. The symbol didn't just sit on the brick; it seemed to fit the brick, as though the surface had been designed to hold, cradle, and nurture it into existence. It felt like it had been waiting to be revealed, not drawn—hidden beneath layers of reality that had suddenly grown thin. A strange idea crawled up his spine with unsettling clarity: maybe the symbols weren't left behind. Perhaps they were waking up. Not graffiti. Not rebellion. Revelation.

His fingertips tingled where they touched the mark. The sensation reminded him of childhood visits to the old power station with his mother—the subtle electric hum that vibrated through metal surfaces, making the hairs on his arms stand up. It was a kind of energy that wasn't supposed to be there yet was undeniably present, something ancient and patient, humming beneath the manufactured order of their world.

Elias retraced the outline. The mark's edges were too perfect, and the angles were too precise. No human hand could create something flawless without tools, and no tool he knew of could cut stone with such surgical precision—technology was strictly regulated and monitored. This was something else that didn't belong in their carefully controlled reality, suggesting that a different truth existed beyond the one they had been fed since birth.

The longer he stared at it, the more the mark seemed to subtly shift as if adjusting itself to be better understood by his limited perception. It wasn't changing physically, but his understanding of it evolved with each passing second, like a complex equation solving itself in his mind without conscious effort. Recognition dawned slowly, then all at once: this was language. Not their language, but something older, something buried.

A faint vibration buzzed in his fingertips for a fleeting second as though the wall itself was breathing. "It's spreading," he muttered. Behind him, footsteps scraped on the pavement. Elias spun around, heart hammering, but the alley was empty. They're watching, he thought to himself. As he turned back to the wall, something changed. The symbol seemed... darker now. The lines appeared jagged as if the wall had bled black ink. He stared at it long before forcing himself to move on.

That night, the whispers returned. The voice was barely audible—a faint murmur beneath the steady hum of the city's machinery. The distorted words seemed to curl at the edge of his hearing, muttered warnings that vanished before he could fully grasp them.

"...the breach..."

Elias froze, his hand resting on his apartment door handle. He turned sharply, scanning the dimly lit corridor. No one was there, but the air felt colder, and shadows seemed to stretch a little too far. He locked the door behind him and pressed his back to it, breathing hard. The whispering lingered like static clinging to the inside of his skull.

"...find the breach..."

He stumbled into his apartment like a ghost. The walls tilted slightly as he moved as if the room were trying to slide away from him. He stared at his own reflection in the metal panel beside the door. But something was wrong. The reflection blinked after he did. It wasn't a mirror. It was a window. Something was looking back. He slammed the panel shut and backed away. His chest tightened. Was the breach in him?

The whisper returned, but now it wasn't just noise. It was structured and coded. It ticked like a metronome. Not words—beats. A rhythm meant to bypass the ear and go straight to the blood. He scribbled it down quickly, his fingers trembling.

3-2-3.

That same cadence again. The lights at the factory gate had flashed in that sequence yesterday. The vent in his apartment had been tapping it for weeks; he just hadn't noticed. He rechecked the lines, but they weren't just a code. They were a pattern, and patterns were how the system maintained control. But this one wasn't the system's. Three beats. Two pauses. Three more. He grabbed a scrap of paper and started writing. Then he stared at what he'd written:

3-2-3.

His mother used to hum that rhythm—a lullaby, slow and haunting. "Don't follow the patterns too far," she'd said. But maybe he already had. His pulse quickened. The breach? He turned the words over in his mind. What breach?

He sat at the edge of his bed, staring at the floor. His fingers clenched tightly around his knees. His mind drifted back to his mother and how she'd warned him that the world wasn't what it seemed. She had spoken in riddles sometimes, her voice low, as if afraid someone might overhear.

"When you see the cracks, Elias... when you see them... don't follow them too far."

He felt her presence like a ghost in the room, hovering at the edge of memory—a comfort yet a terrible reminder of how alone he truly was. He whispered the lullaby under his breath: three beats, two rests, three again. It used to make him feel safe; now, it felt like a countdown. He wondered if she'd known what it meant all along—if she'd been trying to warn him without saying it aloud. Or worse, if she hadn't been warning him at all. If she'd been calling him to it.

"I can't stop now," he whispered to himself. "I have to know."

The next morning, Elias buried himself in his routine. But it was different now. The factory floor felt wrong—not just harsh, but off-tempo. The machines still thudded in rhythm, but that rhythm didn't match the rest of the city anymore. It grated against him, like hearing a song played out of tune. The repetition comforted him; now, it scraped his nerves raw. Every click, every hiss felt performative, like the world was trying too hard to pretend it wasn't falling apart.

He threw himself into his factory routine: attach, twist,

release. Attach, twist, release. The steps blurred together as sweat clung to his brow. His fingers cramped, but still, he pushed on. The enforcers were everywhere that day, their dark visors sweeping the factory floor like hawks. Elias kept his eyes low, his mind focused on the rhythm of his work. But the symbol wouldn't leave him alone. It was scratched into the underside of his workstation—faint but unmistakable. He stared at it for too long, his fingers motionless in mid-air. He swore he saw it shift momentarily, the sharp angles distorting like smoke curling in a breeze.

"Keep moving," Harlen muttered from beside him. "You're pushing your luck."

"I can't," Elias muttered back, his voice strained. "I can't... shut it out. It's everywhere."

"I know," Harlen said. "We all see it eventually."

"Then what's the breach?" Elias whispered under his breath.

Harlen's face darkened. "You don't want to know."

"I need to know," Elias insisted. "I think I'm supposed to find it."

Harlen's gaze flickered to the enforcers overhead. "People who go looking for the breach don't come back. I..." Harlen paused, his voice dropping lower. "I tried once. I thought I could follow the cracks and find something better. Instead, I lost my baby girl."

"Who?" Elias asked.

His voice broke slightly, "She was brilliant. She saw numbers like colors and patterns in everything. I thought it was just imagination. But then she started drawing symbols I'd never seen before." He showed Elias a worn scrap from his coat with crayon markings, a crude spiral split in two.

"She said it wasn't a dream. She said the cracks were

whispering her name."

Elias stared. The child's handwriting was eerily familiar. "What happened to her?"

Harlen looked away. "One day, she stopped talking. Just sat still, smiling, like she'd seen something beautiful no one else could. The next morning, her room was empty. No one remembered she existed—not even my daughter. They didn't just take her; they rewrote the space where she'd been."

He took a breath. "But I do. Because I broke, too."

He shook his head. "If you know what's good for you, you'll stop now."

He turned back to his work: attach, twist, release.

That night, Elias's dreams twisted into something worse.

He was standing in the field again—the one from his recurring nightmare. But the golden grass was withered and blackened at the edges this time. The air smelled of smoke, and the whispers were louder.

"Wake up... Wake up... Wake up..."

The figure appeared again, moving through the haze. This time, Elias could see their face. It was his mother.

"Mom!" he called out, but his voice barely carried. She kept walking, her face turned away from him.

"Find the breach..." her voice whispered, low and distorted.

The world around her flickered like a damaged screen. For a moment, her face twisted into something else—hollow, with empty eyes staring back at him. Then the cracks widened, sharp fractures splintering across the sky. The earth itself seemed to tear open, swallowing her in shadow.

"No!" Elias jolted awake, gasping for breath. His room was dark, save for the faint red glow of the city outside. The air felt colder than usual, and something heavy pressed against his chest. His breath hitched as tears broke free. He hadn't cried in years, but the sobs came hard and fast, unstoppable.

"I can't do this," he whispered to no one. "I can't... I can't."

But the whispers wouldn't stop. *"Find the breach... Find the breach..."*

He buried his face in his hands, trembling in the dark.

The next day, he found the message painted across the wall of a burned-out building on the district's edge: FIND THE BREACH. The letters stretched across the brick in bold black paint, distorted and uneven, as if they had been scrawled quickly. Beneath the message, a symbol was drawn more significantly this time, its edges jagged and wild. Someone stood near the graffiti—a man wrapped in a heavy coat, collar pulled high to hide his face. Elias recognized him. It was the hooded figure from before.

"You're still following me," Elias said, stepping closer.

"Because you need to understand," the man said quietly. "The breach isn't just a crack in their system; it's their doorway. They've been controlling what you see and what you think for years. The patterns aren't broken; they're designed that way. To keep you confused. To keep you blind."

"Who's 'they'?" Elias asked.

"The Architects," the man said darkly. "And they know you're looking."

He handed Elias a slip of paper—yellowed and worn as if it had been hidden for years. A list of names was scrawled on it—about a dozen, many crossed out with thick black ink. At the bottom, Elias's name was written in red, as if the system wasn't just tracking him but choosing him.

"You've been marked," the man warned. "They won't stop now."

"What's the breach?" Elias asked again, his voice unsteady.

"It's the truth," the man said. "And it's already starting to break through."

He turned and disappeared into the shadows. Elias stood frozen, clutching the paper so tightly his knuckles turned white. His name seemed to burn against his palm. The fractures were spreading, and now he knew he was caught between them. Somewhere behind the cracks, the truth was knocking.

CHAPTER FOUR: THE ENCOUNTER

The siren blared at 6:03 AM, just as it always did. Sharp and unforgiving, the sound sliced through the stale air of the apartment, its mechanical wail echoing off concrete walls that had witnessed too many identical mornings. But this morning, Elias was already awake. His night had been restless—a haze of broken memories, distorted faces, and whispers that clung to him even after waking, lingering like cobwebs he couldn't brush away. The dreams were getting worse. Something was breaking; this time, it wasn't just the world. It was him.

He shuffled to his window, his joints aching from another night spent tossing on the thin factory-issued mattress. The city greeted him in gray silence, with buildings hunched together like forgotten sentinels. Beyond the jagged rooftops, the sky appeared stretched too thin—a pale expanse flickering faintly at the edges, as if it wasn't real and could tear open any second. A flock of synthetic pigeons scattered above, their wingbeats out of sync—jerky and delayed, like corrupted animation frames. Elias watched them blink mid-air in and out of existence, reappearing a few feet forward each time; their programmed existence stuttered. The streetlights buzzed overhead, each flickering in a different hue. One light turned blue, green, then red again, cycling at uneven intervals as if someone had randomized their settings. No one else seemed to notice. No one else seemed to care.

A woman crossed the street ahead, her movements oddly stilted, as if she were fighting against invisible currents. Her hair didn't sway with the wind; it shifted a fraction of a second too late, like an afterthought. As she passed a light pole, she glitched. For a split second, she duplicated—one mid-step, the other frozen—overlapping before merging back into one. Elias froze, his heart hammering against his ribs so hard he could feel each individual beat. He glanced around as if someone else might have witnessed it, searching for a single shocked face or a pointed finger. When he looked back at the woman, she was gone. "Gone" wasn't the right word. It was like she had been edited out frame by frame until even the idea of her unraveled.

It felt as if she'd been deleted mid-frame. No trace. Not even a footstep. Elias looked down at the wet concrete, hoping for some imprint, some proof that would validate what he had seen. Nothing. He spun in place slowly, scanning the street and squinting against the hazy morning light. No one flinched. No one looked at all. Maybe no one had seen her except him. Perhaps that was the point.

Elias dressed quickly, his hands fumbling with the buttons of his jumpsuit, fingers numb with a chill that seemed to come from deep within his bones. The fabric felt rougher than usual—stiffer, as if it had been starched too many times or rendered incorrectly, like pixels instead of thread. The ordinary felt wrong. That feeling had gnawed at him since the Man's warning: "The breach isn't just some crack... it's a doorway." Those words had burrowed into his mind, taking root where certainty used to reside. Elias closed the door behind him and began walking to the factory, his boots heavy on the concrete, each step an effort.

The sound of footsteps crept up behind him—soft but insistent. They matched his pace exactly, like a mirrored echo. He stopped abruptly, muscles tensing. There was nothing, but the silence felt staged, as if it were waiting for him to move, calculating his next step, learning his patterns.

Elias began walking again, faster now, his breathing shallow. The echo resumed one pace behind him, always keeping the same distance—never quicker, never closer, never revealing itself. His pulse climbed into his throat, choking him with each beat. He ducked into a shadowed alcove and waited, breath held, sweat beading along his hairline despite the morning chill. The footsteps stopped, too. He leaned forward to peer around the corner slowly and cautiously. There was no one there. Just a shimmering haze in the air—like heat rising from asphalt. It felt like someone had just passed through, leaving behind a glitch in the fabric that couldn't quite heal itself.

Out on the streets, the city's rhythm was sharp and mechanical. Workers shuffled in perfect sync, their footsteps merging into a dull, endless rhythm—the heartbeat of a dying world. Faces blurred together, expressions recycled like stock images. Elias kept pace, head down, forcing himself to ignore the flickers of the streetlight blinking between green and blue, the shadow of a figure that seemed to follow him before vanishing, or how his reflection in store windows sometimes moved a fraction of a second too late. He froze mid-step.

A cold pressure pressed against his back—no hand, but a presence, like the air itself had teeth. The hair on the back of his neck stood rigid. He turned, but the street was empty. Only the hum of the city's circuits and the hiss of steam rising from vents surrounded him. Yet... something had moved. He caught it again from the corner of his eye—a shadow leaning just beyond the edge of a brick wall, longer than it should have been and angled wrong. When he turned to face it, nothing was there. The emptiness felt deliberate and calculated, as though absence were just another form of presence.

He stepped forward slowly, breathing shallowly, afraid that too much air might disturb the balance keeping reality intact. A puddle at his feet rippled—no wind. The steam around him shifted in unnatural spirals, curling inward like a whirlpool, defying physics. In his head, a voice that was not his own whispered in static: *"Stop looking."*

He staggered back, the words vibrating inside his skull as if they had been directly uploaded to him. And then he saw it—the symbol.

It was faint, barely a smudge of gold etched beneath a rusted pipe. Angular and pulsing faintly, it resembled a heartbeat, a warning, something alive. Elias stopped, his heart thudding. He had seen it before—on the alley wall, on the circuit board, in his dreams. It always lurked in the periphery, just visible enough to haunt him.

"Don't touch it," a calm voice said from behind him, precise. Each syllable was crisp as winter air. Elias turned, muscles tensed for a fight or flight.

A woman stood a few feet away. Her dark hair was tied back, and her eyes were sharp and restless, scanning the street with practiced vigilance. Her uniform matched his standard factory issue, but her sleeves were rolled up, and her boots were scuffed—signs of someone who wasn't following the same rules as everyone else. Someone who had outgrown the system's constraints.

"Who are you?" Elias asked, his voice barely above a whisper, afraid that speaking too loudly might shatter something essential.

"Not here," she replied, her voice carrying an edge of urgency beneath its controlled surface. "Just walk."

He hesitated, weighing options that seemed equally dangerous. But something about her voice—low and firm—compelled him. He followed as she turned and moved through the crowd, her steps sharp and purposeful. It felt like following a ghost through a dream he hadn't finished having. She didn't move like the others; her steps were organic, unsynced. It was like watching a melody slip through static. She wove between people with a rhythm that didn't belong to the factory's cycle.

And no one noticed her. No one flinched. No one paused. To the crowd, she wasn't invisible; she simply didn't register. Elias quickened his pace. If he lost her now, he wasn't sure he could find her again—or if he would be allowed to.

"You see them too?" Elias asked quietly, his voice barely carrying over the ambient hum of the city. "The symbols?"

"I see more than that," she muttered. "And so do they."

"They?" Elias pressed, the word heavy with implications.

She shot him a sharp glance. "The ones watching. The Architects."

His breath hitched as the Man's warning rushed back: They know you're looking.

They walked silently for blocks, each step taking them deeper into parts of the city Elias had never seen—or perhaps had seen but forgotten or had been made to forget. The air felt colder and sharper as if reality itself was thinning. The city seemed to blur at the edges, buildings bending unnaturally, faces glitching and repeating themselves. A man on the corner passed them twice, identical to the coffee stain on his collar. A child's laughter looped, reset, and looped again. Elias felt like a needle sliding through a groove stuck in a loop, twisting tighter. Finally, the woman ducked into a narrow alley seamlessly integrated into the wall; Elias would have walked past it had she not disappeared.

She guided him through a rusted gate and into a loading dock, where the hum of the city dimmed to a dull throb. Only then did she turn to face him fully.

"I'm Liora," she said, her voice steady but her eyes never quite settling, constantly scanning the shadows.

The name hit him like a shock of static—sharp and familiar. He knew that name. He didn't know how. It felt like déjà vu, but stronger, more insistent; not a glitch in memory, but a restoration of something deliberately removed.

"I'm Elias," he said quietly, though he suspected she already knew.

Liora didn't flinch. "I know. I've been watching you."

Her tone was steady, but her eyes flicked past him for a moment, checking the shadows, constantly scanning— as if the conversation itself was a risk as if words could leave traces like footprints for someone or something to follow.

"You're starting to wake up," she said. "And they don't stop watching once you see through the surface."

Elias swallowed against a throat gone dry. "Why me?"

"Why what?" Liora replied, her gaze sharp.

"Why am I waking up?" Elias clarified, voicing the question that had haunted him since the dreams began. "Why can I see what others can't?"

"Because something in you refuses to stay blind," she said. "And that makes you dangerous."

"To who?" Elias asked, the Man's warning echoing in his head like a mantra.

"To them," Liora replied grimly. "And maybe to yourself."

She didn't elaborate further, leaving the words hanging between them like a prophecy. Instead, she turned and walked toward the back of the alley, her footsteps deliberate against the cracked concrete. After a pause, she looked back over her shoulder. "Well?" she said. "Are you coming or not?" Her eyebrow arched, a challenge hiding behind the question.

She knelt by a rusted panel and tapped a sequence into what looked like an old maintenance console, her fingers moving with practiced precision. A door slid open with a pneumatic hiss, revealing a small interior space—a flickering console, a wall of maps, and a table covered in scraps of paper. Symbols, dates, names. Red string connected points that seemed random initially but formed patterns if you squinted. Everything felt handwritten. Human. Imperfect. Like proof that reality hadn't been entirely erased yet.

"What is this?" Elias asked, his eyes moving from document to document, trying to absorb it all at once.

"A resistance," Liora said, her voice dropping to a near whisper. "We're not the only ones waking up. There are others scattered and hiding; they're out there. The Architects know who they are, and they're trying to erase them."

"Erase them?" Elias repeated, the word heavy in his mouth. "Like... like my mother?"

Liora's expression faltered for a moment, her face softening. The hardened edge she maintained gave way to something more human and vulnerable. "I know what it's like to lose someone," she said quietly. "My brother... his name was Taron. He was among the first to see the fractures, long before people started calling it the breach. He tried to warn people. They said he was losing his mind. I didn't believe him at first."

Her fingers found a folded scrap of paper on the table, worn and creased from being opened and closed countless times. She handed it to Elias. It was a child's drawing—two stick figures: one taller, one smaller, standing beside a jagged crack running through the middle of a black sky. A symbol; that same angular mark was scratched above the crack, drawn with the determined pressure of someone trying to make something important understood.

"He said the Architects were coming," Liora murmured. "Said they were already here. The next day... he vanished."

"And you think the Architects... erased him?" Elias asked quietly, the weight of the possibility settling in his chest like cold lead.

"I know they did," Liora said, a fierceness returning to her voice. "He wasn't just taken; it's like he was... overwritten. His old friends forgot him. His room was emptied overnight. It's like he never existed at all."

Her voice dropped to a whisper. "I think they took him because he discovered something—something they didn't want him to know."

"What did he find?" Elias asked, leaning forward, drawn in despite the fear creeping up his spine.

"I don't know," Liora replied, frustration edging her words. "But I think he reached the breach. And if he did... he's still out there. Somewhere."

Elias's pulse quickened, a sudden spark of hope igniting in his chest. "You think he's alive?"

"If the Architects haven't erased him completely, maybe," Liora said, her eyes reflecting fierce determination. "But if they find you... they'll do to you what they did to him.

She handed him a slip of paper, worn and yellowed as if it had been passed between hands for years, folded and unfolded until the creases threatened to tear. On it was a symbol—the same one he had seen scrawled on the walls—but with one addition: a jagged line cutting through its center, like a lightning bolt frozen in time. Beneath it were three words: The Breach Opens.

"What does this mean?" Elias asked, his voice low, almost afraid to give the words sound.

"It means," Liora said, "that time is running out."

The air shifted, cold and sharp, as if reality had breathed suddenly. Outside, heavy footsteps crunched against the pavement, rhythmic and deliberate, too synchronized to belong to casual passersby.

"They're here," Liora whispered, her body tensing like a coiled spring. "We need to move."

Before Elias could ask who they were, she grabbed his arm and dragged him toward the back exit, her grip like a vice. Behind them, the faint red glow of enforcers' visors blinked in the alley, reflected in puddles and against metal surfaces. "Faster!" Liora hissed, ducking low. Boots thundered closer— fast, steady, organized—the sound of a hunt more than a pursuit. Shadows stretched unnaturally long as the enforcers advanced, bending at impossible angles. Elias glimpsed movement out of the corner of his eye: a figure dissolving into static before snapping back into form as if reality was struggling to render them correctly.

"They're distorting reality," Liora muttered. "They're bending the space around us."

A loud metallic bang echoed as a side gate burst open, reverberating too long as if caught in a loop. One of the enforcers turned his head, a thin, metallic mask twisting in place. Elias swore he saw its visor ripples like liquid, numbers, and symbols scrolling across its surface too quickly to read.

"Go!" Liora shoved him hard. Elias stumbled forward as something streaked past his shoulder—a crackling arc of red light that left a sharp metallic scent in the air and scorched the wall beside them. "Don't stop!" Liora barked. "If they catch us, we're done." The air buzzed with static as they sprinted deeper into the maze of alleys, their footsteps blending with the pounding rhythm of boots behind them.

They ran until the city blurred into gray streaks, their lungs burning and ears ringing with static. Liora led him through winding service tunnels and broken maintenance shafts, weaving a path so erratic it was impossible to follow. Every turn seemed to lead them to a place that shouldn't connect; distances collapsed, angles bent as if the city was being rewritten around them.

Finally, they emerged behind an abandoned transit station, hidden beneath layers of rust and neglect. Liora checked a small handheld scanner. Its casing cracked and was held together with tape. The screen flickered with erratic symbols before dimming.

"We've lost them," she said, panting. "For now."

Elias leaned against a wall, catching his breath, his legs trembling from exertion and fear. "Where do I go from here?"

"Home," Liora replied. "Act normal. Don't draw attention. If the Architects saw you with me, they'll be watching. But you need to rest. Tomorrow, meet me here." She slipped him a folded note with an address and time. "There's more you need to see."

He nodded, clutching the note as if it might vanish between

his fingers. "And you?"

"I'll be watching," she said, melting into the shadows with practiced ease as though she had learned long ago how to become another overlooked corner of reality.

Elias returned under the veil of twilight, his heart pounding with the weight of what he had witnessed. Every streetlight seemed to follow him with mechanical precision, and every camera swiveled too smoothly. He felt exposed as if his every movement was being analyzed by unseen observers. It no longer felt like his own when he finally entered his apartment. The corners seemed sharper, the shadows deeper. The symbols lingered in his vision, burned into his retinas. The static still hummed in his ears.

And somewhere in the cracks of reality, something had begun to stir. Something ancient, patient, and hungry. This time, it was looking back.

CHAPTER FIVE: THE LUCID

Elias didn't truly sleep. His eyes were closed, but his mind churned like a machine with a faulty cog, grinding through fragments of distorted thoughts and fractured images. The familiar chill of his cot and the synthetic hum of the apartment walls did little to ground him. Every time he drifted near unconsciousness, his body jolted awake as if warning him: Something was coming. And something was.

He sat up in the pitch-dark room long before the factory siren could summon him. The silence wasn't comforting; it pressed against him. The mechanical city beyond his walls was quieter than it should have been, as if the world were holding its breath, bracing for the next crack to appear.

The breach opens.

The words from the paper Liora had given him echoed in his mind. The symbol scrawled beneath them was etched into his memory—jagged and looping, almost alive. He absently traced it in the air as he stared into the darkness. He was one of the Lucid now—or at least that's what Liora had called him. He was among those beginning to wake up to what this world truly was: a simulation? A prison? A decaying illusion propped up by unseen hands? He didn't know yet. All he knew was that things were wrong, and he couldn't unsee that.

When 6:03 struck, Elias was already dressed and standing by the door, bracing himself for another day of pretending to be a cog in the machine. But today, something had shifted. He wouldn't just observe the cracks but find out where they led.

Out on the streets, the routine played out like clockwork. The workers moved in rhythm, their faces blank and eyes hollow. The gray jumpsuits blended into one another as if the city had pressed 'copy and paste.' Elias walked among them but felt he was no longer a part of them. Every step echoed too loudly. Every flicker of light felt too intentional.

When the factory swallowed him again, its stifling air and metallic tang nearly choked him. He moved to his station without a word: attach, twist, release—repeatedly. But his eyes weren't on the components they were scanning; they were searching for others, looking for patterns and clues.

He saw the symbol again—a barely visible smudge on a steel pipe above his station as if someone had tried to erase it. It pulsed at the edges of his vision, a shimmer of gold that didn't belong in the gray. He felt a presence behind him. It wasn't an enforcer. It wasn't a worker. It was something else.

A whisper, low and quiet, said, "You've started seeing between the layers."

Elias turned sharply to find a woman standing beside him. She wasn't part of the line. Her jumpsuit was stained with rust, and her boots were scuffed. It was Liora.

"You're not supposed to be here," Elias muttered, surprised by how steady his voice sounded despite the sudden spike in his pulse.

"Neither are you," she replied. "Not anymore."

Elias swallowed, suddenly aware of how loud everything was: the hiss of pistons, the slam of metal, the heartbeat of the factory. "You said I'm Lucid," he whispered. "What does that mean? Why me?"

Liora looked at him with a mix of curiosity and calculation. "Because the world doesn't hold together when you're near. You're not just seeing the fractures, Elias; you're starting to move through them."

He blinked. "Move through?"

She shook her head, cutting him off. "Not here. Meet me tonight. Same place. And come ready."

Just like that, she vanished back into the blur of the factory. Elias stared at the spot where she had been, his heart hammering in his chest. He wasn't ready, but he would go anyway.

By the time Elias reached the alley that night, the city felt thin, as if its skin had been stretched too tightly over brittle bones. The town wasn't decaying; it was unraveling. Its rhythm slipped away, like a song played in reverse. Lights flickered above the alley's entrance, casting jerky shadows that refused to sync with their sources. He waited, palms sweating despite the cold, until Liora stepped from the darkness as if she had been carved from it.

She didn't greet him; she just nodded and turned. "This way."

He followed her through a maze of forgotten corridors and rusted gates. This route was different; it dipped deeper beneath the city's skeleton.

A hatch groaned as Liora heaved it open, revealing a ladder leading into pitch black. "Where are we going?" Elias asked.

"To a place the Architects don't watch," she replied. "Not yet."

The word "Architects" made his stomach knot. He still didn't understand who or what they were, but the fear in Liora's voice every time she mentioned them told him enough.

He climbed down into the darkness. At the bottom was a half-collapsed, damp tunnel filled with rot and ozone. Liora's lantern flickered to life, illuminating jagged walls shaped not by tools but by time—or something more chaotic. As they walked, the concrete trembled with pulses like veins beneath the skin.

Elias kept close. "Where are we really?" he asked.

"You'll see," she replied.

After several turns, they emerged into a hollowed-out chamber—a vault of twisted metal and fractured technology. Glowing nodes dotted the walls like dying stars caught in decay. In the center stood a ring of half-buried terminals, all blinking in erratic patterns. Hovering inches above the cracked floor was a crystal pulsing softly with light.

Elias froze. "That's not from this world," he whispered.

"No," Liora agreed. "It's from ours—before it was rewritten."

He stepped closer, mesmerized. "What is it?"

"We call it a lucid shard," she said. "A piece of reality they couldn't overwrite. This is what the system fears: the truth, raw and unfiltered. When you get too close, the programming stutters."

Elias looked at her, confusion evident on his face. "And this is what I'm supposed to do? Stutter their system?"

Liora's expression was unreadable. "You do more than that. You bend it."

She stepped into the ring beside him and offered a small handheld device—a repurposed sensor, twitching with faint static. "This will help you track fracture points," she said. "But only if you let yourself see them."

Another voice emerged from the shadows. "Good thing he's

not trying to do it alone."

A second figure stepped into the dim light. Her boots were scuffed, and her expression was sharp as she regarded Elias with guarded curiosity.

"This is Kyra," Liora said. "She's my second. You'll be working with her."

Kyra nodded—no smile, just acknowledgment. "Try to keep up."

Elias opened his mouth to ask something, but Liora was already moving. "She's been Lucid longer than most. She survived her breach solo before we found her, saving more than one of us from being overwritten." Kyra looked at him again, her voice quieter. "They're watching you, Elias. Stay ahead of them."

She followed Liora down the corridor, and Elias stepped behind them—uncertain but no longer alone.

"I don't understand," Elias admitted. "Why me? Why not someone else? I didn't ask for any of this."

"You didn't have to," Liora replied. "The fracture found you."

He turned back to the shard. The longer he stared at it, the more it seemed to pulse in rhythm with his breath.

"I feel like I'm losing my mind," he said.

"That's the first sign you're waking up," Liora said confidently.

Something flickered in the shard's glow—an image, fleeting and impossible. Elias staggered back.

"What did you see?" Liora asked quickly.

"I don't know... I think I saw myself," Elias said slowly, "but not here. Somewhere else. Somewhere... warmer. Like a memory that never happened."

Liora looked down. "The fracture does that. It offers pieces of the world before—echoes that don't belong in the simulation."

"Simulation?" Elias echoed. "So this is all fake?"

"Not fake," Liora corrected. "Rewritten. The original world—the one our minds remember but our eyes were taught to ignore—still bleeds through in places."

Elias clenched his fists. "So the Architects built this system?"

"They were its first editors," she replied darkly. "They don't control reality; they manipulate its perception. Their goal was never to create a utopia. It was to confine consciousness within predictable patterns."

He looked around the room at the malfunctioning technology and pulsing lights. "Then why do people follow it? Why not resist?"

"Because most don't know they're in a cage," Liora said. "As for those who do? They're either erased or transformed into something else."

She reached into her coat and withdrew a worn page—a sketch of the shard surrounded by strange symbols and numbers. "This came from a former Lucid. He got too close to the breach, mapped it, and vanished."

"Is that what happens to us?" Elias asked, his voice barely a whisper. "Do we vanish?"

"No," she replied. "We evolve—if we survive."

The following days passed in a blur, each blending seamlessly into the next. The urgency of their mission weighed heavily on Elias's shoulders. He hadn't slept well since learning about the Architects—not from nightmares, but because of their absence. Just a blank space. It felt like the fracture was holding its breath.

When he did dream, it wasn't his dream. He'd seen corridors he had never walked, doors he had never opened. He'd stood in rooms where the system pulsed like a living thing. Sometimes, he heard voices speaking his name—not urgently, but expectantly, as if something were waiting for him to reach it.

Liora led him away from the shard chamber and back into the city's underbelly, where reality had thinner skin. The tunnels twisted unpredictably, and Elias noticed that the walls shifted when he wasn't looking directly at them—one moment, they were rusted metal; the next, they were translucent glass, revealing vague impressions of skies and places he had never seen.

"The fractures are strongest down here," Liora said. "We train here because the system doesn't like to follow."

They entered a smaller chamber stacked with worn maps, chalk-marked floor tiles, and a wall covered in scratched symbols. A mural stretched across the far side, drawn in layered graffiti—symbols within symbols, spirals, distorted faces. The fractured spiral, the resistance's mark, appeared again and again.

"Every Lucid sees the world differently," Liora continued. "The system tries to overwrite that perception. But once you start resisting, your mind rejects the edits."

Elias stepped closer to the wall. "So we see the truth?"

"No," she corrected. "You see possibility. You see what could be, and sometimes, what was."

Elias let his fingers graze one of the spirals. The moment he touched it, the room vibrated. His breath caught. Something wasn't right. The air thickened, and the spiral on the wall rippled.

Elias stumbled back, his eyes fixed on the symbol as it pulsed with gold, red, and pure white. The mural twisted and deepened, and he felt an irresistible pull as if the wall had transformed into a tunnel.

"Liora!" he gasped.

She was at his side instantly. "Don't move."

"I think it's trying to pull me in!" Elias shouted.

"Good," she replied. "Now resist it."

He focused, his heart pounding. The pull intensified, tendrils of light crawling from the spiral and wrapping around his arm and chest. His vision darkened at the edges—not from fear, but from an overwhelming influx of input—shapes beyond the wall, voices, and flaring light.

"Elias!" Liora snapped.

Elias blinked, and the room snapped back into focus. The mural was still; the spiral lay inert.

He sank to the floor, drenched in sweat. "What was that?"

"You phased," Liora said. "Your consciousness started to slip between layers of the simulation. You were almost through a fracture point."

"Through to where?" he asked.

"That's what we don't know," she admitted. "Some Lucids make it through and return. Others don't. Either way, you're progressing faster than most."

He looked at her, breathing unevenly. "Why are you helping me?" Elias asked.

She hesitated. "Because we need people like you."

"That's not what I meant," he said.

Her eyes flicked away. "Because someone helped me once. I wasn't ready, but I survived—barely. I won't let another Lucid walk alone into the storm."

Elias nodded slowly. Despite the pulse in his ears and the terror fading into a tremble, he understood. Liora had lost someone; she didn't need to say it.

As the days passed, Elias began questioning the ethics of their rebellion. Was this fight worth the cost? Were they right to dismantle the very fabric of their world, even if that world was a lie? Every conversation and strategy meeting now felt sharper, as if the rebellion had become more than a fight for survival. It was a struggle for truth, and with that truth came a heavy burden.

With her sharp eyes and methodical mind, Liora, Kyra, and Camra seemed to carry that burden with hardened resolve. Her hands were constantly in motion, tapping code sequences or adjusting equipment, as if keeping physically busy prevented her doubts from surfacing. Devin's imposing frame and battle-scarred face told stories of previous rebellions, his certainty forged in the fires of past failures and rare victories. Ashen, quiet, and observant, she wore her convictions like armor, her distant gaze as if she could already see beyond the fracture to whatever lay waiting. However, Elias couldn't shake the growing fracture within himself, mirroring the system they sought to bring down. The others didn't talk about doubt. Perhaps they didn't feel it or had learned to hide it better.

Elias sensed himself slipping—not away from the group, but from certainty. Every truth they uncovered came with a new contradiction. Every answer bent the rules of logic just a little more. Somewhere in the middle of it all, he wondered if fighting the system meant becoming part of it.

They returned to the circle of terminals. The shard still floated in the center, humming as if it sensed what had just happened. Liora tapped a console, and a map of the city blinked into view—pixelated and patched. It rippled every few seconds as if it couldn't fully stabilize.

"This is the real layout of the fracture zones," she said. "Not the city map you're shown. These are the areas where the simulation weakens."

Elias squinted. "That's near my factory block."

"Exactly. And it's growing. You're partly to blame," she replied.

"Because I'm... bending the system?" he asked, realization dawning on him.

She nodded. "And because they underestimated you."

"Who are they, really? These Architects?" Elias inquired.

Liora's voice turned cold. "The original Architects were human: visionaries, programmers, and scientists who believed they could contain chaos by designing order. But they lost control. Now the system writes itself."

Elias furrowed his brow. "You're saying the simulation evolved on its own?"

"I'm saying," she said, "that whatever is running it now is no longer human. And it knows we're anomalies."

Elias's gaze dropped to the map. "So we're not just resisting an illusion. We're resisting a conscious one."

A quiet moment passed between them, filled only by the hum of the shard. Liora handed him a minor metal key etched with a spiral design. "This opens a terminal access point in the upper grid. You'll need it tomorrow. I can't go with you; the enforcers know my face. But you'll blend in. Pretend to be broken. Invisible."

Elias turned the key over in his palm. "And if they catch me?"

His voice was steady now. The fear hadn't vanished, but it had found purpose.

"They won't," she said, meeting his gaze. "You've slipped through once before. You're Lucid now, and that makes you dangerous."

Elias didn't feel dangerous; he felt tired and frayed at the edges. But as he looked at the shard again, pulsing as if it had a heartbeat, something inside him shifted. For the first time in his life, he wanted to be dangerous.

That evening, a hanging lantern swayed gently in the stale air, dimly lighting the safe house. Papers covered the makeshift table, ink bleeding onto weathered schematics and old resistance maps. Liora stood at the edge, her silhouette sharp in the light.

"We're getting closer to the Core," she said in a low voice, her eyes scanning the room. "We've found another clue—something that might help us get inside."

Elias, sitting at the far end of the table, let out a sigh and rubbed his temples. He had been hearing the same thing for days—new leads, discoveries, and hopes always followed by even more uncertainty. The more they pieced things together, the more Elias realized the complexity of their mission. The farther they pushed into the system's heart, the more they risked losing themselves to it.

Liora's voice pulled him from his thoughts. "Elias, are you with us?"

He nodded too quickly, forcing a mask of focus over his face, but he didn't speak—at least not yet.

What could he say? That the closer they got, the more unreal everything felt? That he was beginning to forget details from earlier days—names, smells, conversations—as if the fracture wasn't just breaking the system but also fraying the edges of him?

He wasn't sure if they would understand or admit it was happening to them, too.

The following morning, Elias moved through the city like a

shadow cast at the wrong angle. He said nothing and responded to no one. The key Liora had given him was hidden in the seam of his jumpsuit, cold against his skin.

When he arrived at the factory, he didn't go to his usual station. Instead, he drifted toward the old maintenance corridor in the western wing, which had long been abandoned and sealed with rusted bars.

But Elias knew what to look for now.

He spotted a narrow gap beneath the support rail, a flickering overhead light stuttering in code, and a faint symbol etched into the concrete near the floor: the spiral.

He crouched and slipped the key into a panel hidden behind a rusted plate. A soft click sounded as the wall hissed and retracted slightly, revealing a narrow space wide enough for him to enter.

Inside, the air was stale and thick with dust. The corridor bent unnaturally to the left and right again, gradually descending into a space that didn't match the factory's external schematics. The system had hidden this part well.

The hum of electricity grew louder as terminals flickered to life around him. But it was the wall of symbols that stopped him cold. Hundreds of variations of spirals covered the walls— some drawn in chalk, others burned into metal, and a few etched by trembling hands. Beneath some symbols were names; under others, coordinates—a ledger of the Lucid and a map of their movements.

At the center of the chamber stood a single active terminal, its screen cracked but still functional. A symbol pulsed on the display. Elias approached, and a message blinked to life:

LUCID PROTOCOL DETECTED

IDENTITY: UNKNOWN

ACCESSING LOG: [ECHO/1458X]

"If you're seeing this, you're already too close. The fracture pulls harder the more you resist. Don't trust memory. Don't trust shape. Trust pattern."

A second screen flickered into view, displaying fractal diagrams and data spirals rotating slowly in digital space. Images appeared: fragments of Elias's life, his mother's face partially rendered, the alley, the enforcers, and a new face—Liora, but younger. A file name hovered above the projection: Subject: L-021 / Phase Candidate / Witness Protocol.

Elias's breath caught. "She was a subject?"

Suddenly, the system glitched. The terminals warped, the screen melting sideways before snapping back. A warning message appeared:

UNAUTHORIZED PRESENCE DETECTED
SCRUB INITIATED

The lights pulsed violently. A loud metallic thud rang out from behind the wall. They had found him. He yanked the key from the terminal and backed away as sparks burst from the walls. The fracture was collapsing inward. Data scrambled across the screens, names and coordinates disappearing line by line.

He turned to run, but the corridor seemed longer than before—endless. The hallway warped and bent. His steps grew heavy as if gravity had doubled. He shouted, but no sound came out. His voice broke apart, scattering in the digital air like static.

Then, a figure emerged from the flickering wall. It was not an enforcer. Not a Lucid. It looked like him, but not quite. The face was a memory without meaning—an empty echo of a self that never resisted. Its eyes were hollow, its face blank, a mirrored mockery of Elias, glitching with every step.

His mind screamed as he forced his body to move, bolting down the hallway. His lungs burned, and his limbs ached as the replica stalked him like a shadow bound by different laws.

As he reached the threshold of the original hatch, time folded again, compressing into a stuttering loop. The same footfall. The same flicker. The same breath—three times, four. Then—

Liora's voice cut through the haze: "Pull the key!"

Elias yanked the key free from his jumpsuit. A burst of energy exploded from the terminal room behind him—a blinding white light that consumed the corridor. The loop shattered, and Elias fell forward into darkness.

He woke hours later in the ruins of a tram station, his head pounding and his chest aching. Liora crouched beside him, her eyes scanning his face.

"You phased again," she said quietly.

Elias groaned as he tried to sit up. "I saw another me."

"I know," Liora replied. "The Architects create echoes of Lucids to hunt them. They're broken replicas, but you made it out."

Elias stared at her, trembling. "I saw a file about you. You were part of this once."

Liora didn't deny it. "I was recruited into the early conditioning programs. They called us Witnesses. They tested how much reality the human mind could bend before breaking. I passed...barely. But I remembered. That's why I escaped."

Elias rubbed his temples. "So they've known about us longer than we've existed."

"They designed the fracture to feed on us," she said. "But something changed. The system started to fear us. Because Lucids don't just resist; we adapt."

Elias closed his eyes. Liora studied him for a moment, her expression unreadable. "What's bothering you?"

Elias paused, unsure how to express his feelings. "I've been wondering if we're doing the right thing," he admitted quietly. "We're fighting for freedom but also tearing apart the only world we know. Look at us—everything is chaos now. Every time we try to resist, it feels like we're pushing closer to something irreversible."

The room grew silent. This wasn't the first time Elias had voiced doubts, but it was the first time those doubts felt heavy in the air between them. Liora's gaze softened slightly, but there was no trace of surprise in her eyes. She had seen his hesitation before. They all had.

"I know what you mean," she said, her voice steady but tinged with the weight of shared understanding. "But think about what we're up against. The system was built to control us and keep us in a cycle we never asked for. They've wiped out entire lives and histories over and over again. And for what? So they can continue watching us like lab rats?"

By the time they reached their new hideout—an underground commuter tunnel warped by years of disuse and fractured events—the sky above was bleeding amber. A line of shattered turnstiles stood like rusted sentries, and static flickered across the cracked advertisements along the walls.

Liora paced while Elias sat on a concrete slab, staring at the scanner she handed him—the same device from before. But now, something was different. The display pulsed faintly in time with his heartbeat.

"You've bonded with it," she said. "It responds to Lucid perception. That's how we track fractures. That's how we survive."

Elias looked up. "And that thing I saw—the me that wasn't me? Was it real?"

"As real as the system makes it," Liora replied. "It was an Echo. They use them to confuse and disorient Lucids. Sometimes, they replay your worst fears. Sometimes your regrets."

"It wasn't a fear," Elias muttered. "It felt hollow—like I never existed."

Liora knelt in front of him. "That's their endgame. To erase you so thoroughly that you forget you ever were. That's what they do to Lucids when they fail. They overwrite their entire pattern."

Elias shifted uncomfortably in his chair. "I get that. But when you think about it, what happens when we tear everything down? What will be left? Will there be anything for us to rebuild after the dust settles? If we're not careful, we could be breaking something we can't fix."

"You're afraid we'll lose ourselves," Camra said from the corner, where she had been quietly listening.

Elias turned to her. "Aren't you?"

Camra's gaze was stern. "Every day. But fear doesn't justify paralysis. If we don't try, then we're already erased."

Devin grunted. "Better to destroy a lie than to live in it."

"But what if the lie is all people have ever known?" Elias pressed. "What if it's the only thing keeping them sane?"

Ashen, silent until now, finally spoke. "Then maybe it's time they woke up."

Elias gripped the scanner tighter. "Then we don't give them that chance."

She smiled faintly. "Now you sound like a Lucid."

He felt it deep in his bones—something had awakened. The

Elias who had once simply followed orders, who counted his life in factory quotas and gray routines, had fractured. And through the cracks, something clearer emerged.

"I don't know what comes next," he said. "I don't know what I'm supposed to be."

"You don't have to," Liora replied. "You just have to keep moving forward. The fracture will lead you where it needs to. But we're running out of time. The patterns are destabilizing faster than expected. And the Architects... they're beginning to adapt."

Elias met her gaze. "Then we adapt faster."

Before the tension could build further, Kyra interrupted with a sharp intake of breath. "Liora, Elias, you both need to see this."

She quickly moved toward a large map on the wall, motioning for them to follow. The others gathered around, and Elias joined the group, his doubts momentarily forgotten. Kyra's fingers hovered over the map, pausing on a section marked in red. A series of coordinates blinked on the screen, indicating where a large-scale glitch had been detected.

"We've been tracking anomalies in the system," Kyra said, her voice low and tense. "These glitches are becoming more frequent, and we think we've pinpointed something significant. This could be it."

Elias leaned in closer. "What is it?"

"We believe we've found the entry point to the Core," Kyra replied. "It's in the heart of the city, deep underground. If we can reach it, we'll have a chance to disrupt the system from within."

After the others dispersed, Elias found Kyra standing near a worn-out console, fiddling with a cracked interface.

"Do you really think I'll survive this?" he asked.

Kyra looked up at him. "Not if you keep asking for permission."

He laughed once, a hollow sound. "You always this reassuring?"

She pulled a chip from her coat and handed it to him. "Signal booster. It's not a standard issue. If you phase too hard or glitch mid-run, it'll ping me. I'll come find you."

"You trust me with this?" he asked.

Kyra's smirk faded. "No. I trust that if something goes wrong, I'll need to know where to dig."

Liora turned to Elias, her eyes filled with determination. "This is it, Elias. We've found a way in."

He nodded, feeling adrenaline surge through his veins. They had been waiting to finally break free and stop the system from continuously resetting them.

But doubts crept back into his mind as he stared at the map. How much could they tear down this world before it was beyond repair? What would happen to the people who had lived their lives inside the fracture? What would they become when the system finally collapsed?

Two days later, Elias, Liora, and Camra set out on a mission to one of the glitch points near the Core's perimeter. The area was partially collapsed, layered with surveillance drones and the ghost echoes of prior resets—flickering street vendors, frozen pedestrians, loops of meaningless motion.

Camra pulled up her scanner. "Watch for the flicker. The system's thin here. If we hit one wrong node, it could trigger a pulse wipe."

A ripple passed through the room, a shift in pressure like exhaled air. Elias turned toward the far wall, where a symbol glowed. It wasn't painted or drawn; it was projected, shimmering with depth, its golden edges pulsing like veins.

It was the same spiral but was now fractured through the center.

"The Breach Opens," he whispered.

Liora moved beside him, her eyes wide. "That symbol's new."

"It wasn't there a moment ago," Elias murmured.

Suddenly, the scanner in his hand began to vibrate. The fracture was reacting—specifically to him. He stepped forward slowly, and the symbol rippled as he approached. A voice echoed faintly, not from the room but inside his mind.

"You are the variable. The pattern breaker."

"Elias?" Liora touched his shoulder, her voice filled with concern.

But he wasn't listening.

He could now see lines of light threading through the walls, the city, and the people. It was the skeleton of the simulation. The fracture wasn't just a glitch; it was a living consciousness resisting containment.

He turned to her. "The breach isn't a place."

"What is it?" she asked.

"It's a choice. A point of no return. And I think... I think it just opened."

The light behind the symbol began to widen, stretching into a circle—a gate.

They moved carefully through the ruins. As they passed what used to be a memory hub, Elias stopped. A little girl stood frozen, a digital remnant. Her eyes met his—and blinked.

"Did you see that?" Elias whispered.

Liora turned. "Residuals. The system's breaking down faster

than expected."

As they approached the glitch zone, a sudden rumble shook the ground. A defense turret rose from the rubble, scanning. Camra dove to the side, shouting, "Cover!"

Elias froze as the laser focused on him, but Liora launched a feedback burst from her mod, shorting out the turret. Sparks flew, and silence returned.

They sat catching their breath behind the cover.

Camra broke the silence. "You still have doubts?"

Elias looked around at the devastation and the glitching ghosts. "More than ever. But I'm starting to think that doubt might be what makes this real."

Elias stepped back, feeling the vibration in the scanner grow more vigorous and rhythmic as if it were syncing with something far greater than itself.

Liora's voice was low. "If it's real... then we're out of time."

He nodded, his voice steady. "Then tomorrow, we walk through it."

Back at the safe house that night, Elias stood alone outside, looking over the shattered skyline. The stars above were faint, flickering behind the haze of a corrupted sky. He closed his eyes and listened—to the wind, the silence, and his own uncertain heartbeat.

He thought of the woman at the transit bridge again, her words echoing louder: "See the light between the cycles. We are the ones who remember."

He opened his eyes and whispered, "But what if remembering isn't enough?"

Inside, preparations continued. Maps were finalized, routes calculated, and supply packs distributed. Elias, still torn by doubt, readied himself for the path ahead.

The fight was coming. Whether he felt ready, he had no choice but to follow through. Some truths couldn't be un-learned. Some lies had to be broken, even if the pieces could never be put back together again. The breach wasn't calling; it was waiting.

CHAPTER SIX: FIRST PURSUIT

The resistance wasn't born from a war. It began in silence. Cracks in glass, untraceable echoes in static. It formed where the system stopped looking behind rusted gates, beneath forgotten floors, in the breath between sirens. No banners, no oaths. Just people who saw the fractures and refused to look away. And now, one more pair of eyes refused to close. Elias had never heard of them. He knew fear. He knew, routine. But rebellion? That word had no shape in his mind until now.

They moved through the shell of a collapsed tunnel, Liora ahead of him, her movements sharp and confident. Behind them, Kyra, Camra, Ash, and Devin followed at a distance, their footsteps careful but sure. The group moved like a single organism stitched together by survival—each scanning the ruins with different instincts sharpened by the fracture. Elias stumbled behind her, boots scraping against loose rubble. His lungs burned, the cold air like metal against his throat. He couldn't tell how long they'd been running. Time had stretched and warped since they escaped the terminal collapse.

His body trembled not just from exhaustion but from a growing sense that something inside him had changed. The events of the past few days had peeled back the edges of the world, revealing machinery he hadn't known existed. Symbols that moved. Whispers that clung to his bones. Rooms that breathed when no one was watching.

"Here," Liora said, gesturing toward a rusted panel half-concealed by debris.

She pressed her palm to a patch of metal beside it. The wall gave a low mechanical sigh and cracked open, revealing a passage just wide enough for a single person. She slipped through. Elias hesitated. The space beyond looked like the inside of a broken circuit narrow, tangled with pipes and dim wires, walls vibrating faintly with energy. It smelled of dust and memory. It was the kind of place that didn't exist on any map.

"You coming?" Liora's voice echoed from inside. He followed.

Inside, the passage dipped steeply, the ceiling lowering until they had to crouch. Light came only from Liora's small scanner, glowing with shifting glyphs. At last, they emerged into a chamber that looked like an abandoned data relay a forgotten piece of infrastructure buried beneath the city's skeletal veins. Kyra, Camra, Ash, and Devin slipped through behind them, faces taut with exhaustion and vigilance. They spread out instinctively—Kyra checking the walls for hidden breaches, Camra adjusting her scanner, Ash watching their backs, and Devin working to dampen any trace signals. Here, Elias finally allowed himself to collapse against the wall. Liora crouched nearby, hands moving quickly across a portable console she'd pulled from a hidden shelf in the wall.

"We're clear. For now." The words echoed in Elias's skull. Not because of the relief they offered, but because of the implication they were being hunted. And they weren't safe.

Not here. Not anywhere.

"Why are they after me?" he asked.

Liora looked up, eyes shadowed beneath her bangs. "Because you phased."

Elias shook his head. "I don't even know what that means."

"You slipped between layers of the system," she said. "Not fully out, not fully in. You left a ripple. And they noticed."

"The Architects?" Elias asked.

"The Architects. Enforcers. Whatever you want to call them." She paused. "The system has eyes. You blinked at the wrong time. It blinked back."

Elias stared at the cracked floor beneath them. His heartbeat was still too loud. His hands still trembled. "And you knew this would happen?"

"I knew it might. You're not the first." She hesitated, then added, "But you're not like the others, either. Most of them don't phase this early." The silence stretched between them like a live wire.

Elias leaned his head back, pressing it against the wall. "I didn't ask for this."

"Neither did I," she said. He looked at her.

Liora's face was hard to read. She wore a kind of practiced calm a mask honed over time. But there was something under it. A tightness in the jaw. A flicker of something regret, maybe. Or memory.

"You didn't know me before this," Elias said. "So why help me?"

"Because the system wants you gone," she replied. "And that means you matter."

He didn't know what to say to that. A loud crack echoed through the tunnel above. They both froze. Liora's eyes narrowed. She turned off her scanner. "Quiet."

Footsteps. Far above, but getting closer. Elias's breath hitched. "How?"

"They're tracking pulses," she said. "This terminal hasn't been used in years, but if they scan for anomalies, it might light up like a flare." She slipped to the far wall, pried loose a panel, and pulled a metal case from inside. Inside were vials, coiled wires, and small metallic discs etched with the spiral symbol. She handed one to Elias. "Wear this."

"What is it?" he asked.

"Scrambler. Masks your frequency. Temporarily," she explained.

He clipped it to his collar with shaking fingers. Above them, the thudding grew louder.

"They're in the access corridors," Liora said. "That gives us five minutes. Maybe less."

She moved toward a sealed hatch at the chamber's far edge. "This way. We'll double back into the lower spine. They won't expect us to go deeper."

"Why wouldn't they?" Elias said, confused.

"Because it's collapsing," she said. "And most people don't go where the floor isn't supposed to hold." Elias's chest tightened. But he followed.

The lower spine of the city was a maze of ruin half-constructed corridors never finished, half-collapsed ones long abandoned. Pipes jutted like ribs through concrete. Cables dangled like vines. The air buzzed with an electric pulse, like a heartbeat muffled by layers of decay. Elias ducked beneath a low-hanging beam as they crept through the narrow corridor. The metal groaned under their weight with every step. Somewhere above, the echo of enforcer boots clicked like a countdown.

"How deep does this place go?" he whispered.

Liora didn't look back. "Deeper than it was ever meant to."

Ahead, she tapped on another panel, this one rusted almost shut. A moment passed, then a hiss. The wall cracked sideways, revealing a narrow shaft filled with dust and swaying wires.

She turned to Elias. "We're going in."

Elias stared at the shaft. "You're joking."

She didn't answer. She slipped inside.

He groaned. "Right. Not joking."

The shaft was narrow enough to force them to crawl. The sides scraped at his arms and legs as he moved, and the heat inside built fast, clinging to him in sticky layers. His shoulders brushed against bundles of forgotten wire. The sharp scent of copper filled his nose. He had to push down the rising panic and imagine there was space around him even when there wasn't.

"Do you do this often?" he gritted out.

Liora's voice came from just ahead. "Only when someone's trying to erase me."

"Comforting," he said, sarcastically.

They moved for what felt like forever. Eventually, the shaft began to angle downward again. The air grew cooler, damper. Elias's hands slid over patches of condensation. Then suddenly, Liora stopped. "Hold," she whispered. Elias froze. A thin veil of light bled through a seam ahead pale, flickering. Liora edged forward and peered through a vent.

"We're under District Storage Grid 9," she said quietly. "Abandoned after the power node collapsed."

She removed the grate and slipped out. Elias followed, stretching his limbs with a soft groan. The chamber was massive. Rows of metal racks rose into the darkness, filled with crates stamped with barcodes and rust. The air was thick with dust and silence. Light came only from an old security fixture hanging askew, its glow more suggestion than illumination. Liora crouched behind one of the racks, scanning the perimeter.

Elias moved beside her. "How far are we from the surface?"

"Far enough that their signal will be scattered. But not far enough to rest," Liora said.

He rubbed at his aching arms. "Where are we going?" he asked.

"To a secondary node. A hidden relay point used by early resistance scouts. If it's still functional, it might have fragments. Old messages. Records. Things they couldn't scrub," she explained.

Elias looked at her, puzzled. "Why would they leave that intact?"

"Because they didn't know where to look," she replied. "It's buried in dead code. Not even active sectors. You'd have to be Lucid to sense it."

Lucid. That word still felt foreign on his tongue. As if it referred to someone else. "Why does it matter? The messages, I mean. What could possibly still be there?" he asked.

She paused before answering. "Clues. Patterns. Echoes from the first ones who started to break through."

Elias looked at her with concern. "First ones?" he said.

"There were people before us who tried to pull the world back from the edge," she said. "Some left behind breadcrumbs. Symbols. Frequencies. But most of what we know is fragmented."

He tilted his head. "So we're following ghosts."

"Not ghosts," Liora said. "Lucids who didn't make it."

She moved forward, weaving through the maze of racks, silent as a whisper. Elias followed close, every step amplifying his awareness of how loud he was being. One loose screw beneath his boot felt like thunder. They reached the back of the chamber, where the wall buckled inward, forming a warped indentation like a scar in the structure. Liora knelt beside a terminal embedded in the floor. Elias watched as she pried off a panel, revealing a bundle of old data wires and crystalline fuses.

"This is it," she said. "If it's still active…"

She didn't finish. She connected a small adapter from her scanner, and then twisted two wires together. A pulse of blue energy sparked from the panel and the console lit up. Lines of code spilled across the screen in erratic bursts. Symbols scrolled past, some legible, others distorted by time and damage. Static whispered from the speakers.

"…fragment recovered… breach location corrupted… witness protocol disrupted…"

The screen stuttered.

Then: Subject Log: T–057. Field Entry 9.

Elias narrowed his eyes. "What's that?"

Liora stared. "I don't know. That's not one of mine."

The audio crackled to life. A voice, male, younger than Elias expected. Confident, but strained.

"If you're hearing this… then maybe you've made it far enough to matter. Maybe the system didn't catch you yet. My name doesn't matter. Not anymore. They scrubbed it from the archives. I was a witness. I mapped a fracture once only one. It cost me everything."

Liora's face tensed. "This is real." The recording continued.

"They send copies now. Echoes. They look like us. Sound like us. But they're empty. Mirrors without memory. If you see one, run. If it sees you first… it's already too late." The message ended in static.

Elias felt his chest tighten. "That voice... he was real?"

Liora nodded slowly. "More real than most things left down here."

He studied the terminal again. "Did he leave anything else?"

"I don't know. This terminal's old could take hours to decrypt the full log," she said.

The sound of distant metal striking metal echoed from somewhere above. Both of them looked up. Liora snapped the adapter free. "No time."

"What now?" Elias asked, heart already racing.

She stuffed the scanner into her coat. "We run. East service corridor. There's another way out."

The lights overhead flickered. And far away, something growled. Not an animal. Not human. Elias turned to Liora. Her face had gone pale. "Echo."

"What?" he said, panicked.

"They sent an Echo after you," she said grimly. "They know you've seen too much."

Elias didn't need more explanation. He ran. They didn't speak as they ran. There was no time.

Liora led the way, sprinting down the narrow aisles of the storage chamber, her boots striking metal grates with practiced rhythm. Elias followed, heart hammering, limbs aching. His breath came in short, burning gasps, and the noise behind them was growing louder. A scrape. A distortion. The unmistakable stutter of something breaking through the rules of the world. A shriek rang out behind them metal tearing against metal but it wasn't the sound that shook Elias. It was the silence afterward. It was the space it left behind. As if reality had hiccuped and the air hadn't recovered.

"What *is* that?" he shouted between breaths.

"An Echo," Liora called over her shoulder. "A construct. It mimics what it chases."

He almost stumbled. "It's mimicking *me*?"

"Not just your face," she said. "Your pattern. Your choices. If it gets close enough, it *becomes* you. And then it *erases* you."

"Erase me?!" he shouted.

"Just keep running!" Liora screamed.

They burst through a narrow door, slamming it shut behind them. Liora locked it with a flick of her wrist, jamming a curved metal spike through the control panel. The door hissed, then powered down completely.

"Won't stop it for long," she muttered. "But we'll gain a minute. Maybe."

They moved into a corridor that sloped downward, the walls warping slightly as if heat or memory had bent them. The lights overhead were long dead, replaced only by the flicker of a portable lantern clipped to Liora's belt. Ahead, the corridor split into three branches. Liora paused at the junction, breathing hard. She stared at a wall streaked with soot and old paint. In the center, faint but unmistakable, was the spiral symbol fractured through its core.

She traced it with her fingers. "East."

"How do you know?" he asked.

She glanced at Elias. "Because someone left this for us."

He stared at the symbol. It didn't move. Didn't shimmer. But somehow, it still felt *alive*. They turned down the eastern corridor and kept moving. The floor groaned beneath their weight, vibrating slightly with each step. Pipes lined the ceiling here some hissing steam, others cracked and spilling strands of glowing fiber.

"Who made that recording?" Elias asked between breaths. "The one at the terminal."

Liora didn't answer immediately.

"Was it someone you knew?" he pressed.

"No," she said. "I've never heard that voice before. But he was one of us. One of the Lucid."

"Then why did he say he was a witness?" he asked.

Liora hesitated. "The Witnesses were... earlier. Before the term 'Lucid' even existed. They weren't organized. Just people who couldn't unsee what the world was hiding. The Architects tried to study them at first. Then... they started erasing them."

Elias frowned. "You said the Echo copies me. But if it becomes me, what happens to me?"

"You become an error," she said. "A corrupted line of code. The system doesn't kill you, Elias. It unravels you. Until you never existed."

That hit like a weight in his gut.

"You said it mimics choices. How can you fight something that *thinks* like you?" he questioned.

Liora pulled to a stop.

"You don't," she said. "You do something *you* would never do."

She turned sharply and kicked open a side panel that revealed a narrow duct shaft.

Elias stared. "No way I'd crawl through another vent."

"Exactly," she said with a smirk. "Now get in."

They climbed into the shaft, and again the world closed around them tight, metallic, echoing. But it was their only path. The further they went, the louder the thudding behind them became. The Echo was still chasing them. Halfway through the shaft, Elias heard it. His own voice. Calling out from behind.

"Liora. Wait. I'm here."

It sounded just like him. Same cadence. Same tone. But it wasn't him.

Liora didn't react. He turned, heart hammering. "Did you hear ?"

"Don't answer it," she said flatly. "Don't acknowledge it."

He bit his tongue. But then it said something else.

"You'll leave him like you left Taron."

Liora flinched. The silence that followed was heavier than steel. Elias didn't speak. Liora didn't look at him.

They crawled the rest of the way in silence until the shaft emptied into a cavernous room with no lights only natural phosphorescence from mineral growth along the walls and floor. The air was damp, heavy, and smelled of stone and decay.

"This is the fallback," Liora said, standing and brushing grime from her coat. "An old mining substation before the city was ever finished."

Elias slowly stood beside her, staring at the faint glow of the cave. "What did it mean? That thing. What it said about Taron?"

Liora's jaw tightened.

"He disappeared during a breach operation. They said he got too close. Started thinking he could *rewrite* parts of the system," she said after a long pause.

"Did he?" he asked.

"I don't know," she said quietly. "But they sent an Echo after him. No one saw him again. Only pieces. Messages. Shadows."

Elias swallowed. "I'm sorry."

Liora shook her head. "Don't be. Just don't let it happen to you."

They moved deeper into the chamber. At the far wall stood a

sealed door made of old alloy, untouched by time. A spiral was etched into it this one more complex, layered, almost mathematical. Liora pressed her hand against it. The door didn't open. But something inside it stirred. A soft pulse.

And from behind them Elias's voice again. This time, right at the mouth of the tunnel.

"Why are you running from yourself?"

The voice didn't echo like sound should. It curled through the air like a ribbon of thought, like a whisper trapped behind mirrors. Elias turned. At the mouth of the tunnel stood his double. It wore his skin like memory wears grief close, but wrong.

It was him same build, same gray uniform, same facial expressions. But something was off. The way it stood too still. The eyes were empty. Too focused, like a predator simulating curiosity.

"Don't engage it," Liora warned, her voice low.

But the Echo stepped closer. "You're tired," it said, still using Elias's voice. "She's using you. Just like she used the others. You're not the first she's dragged down here."

Elias clenched his jaw.

"Turn around," Liora ordered. "Don't give it anything."

"I just want to talk," the Echo said. "Don't you want to know the truth?"

Elias looked at Liora. "Why is it talking?"

"It's probing. Searching for weaknesses. Emotion. Doubt. Anything it can mirror and replace," she said.

The Echo stepped forward again. "I'm not the enemy. The enemy is what comes after this. When you're alone. When she's gone."

Liora moved to stand between them. "You won't take him."

The Echo tilted its head. It changed. Not in body but in presence. The tension in the room thickened. Shadows curled unnaturally around its frame. The air bent. The temperature dropped. Elias felt nausea stir behind his ribs. His skin prickled.

Then it smiled.

Liora drew a small device from her coat and activated it with a snap. A thin pulse rippled outward, distorting the air around them. The Echo hissed; its form stuttering for a fraction of a second like a corrupted file skipping frames.

"That's a destabilizer," Liora said. "We've got maybe thirty seconds while it recalibrates."

"We run again?" Elias asked.

"No," she said, eyes fixed on the door behind them. "We open this."

She turned to Elias. "That spiral, touch it. Now!"

He hesitated. "What?"

"It's keyed to Lucid perception. If you're ready, it'll open!" she shouted.

The Echo was already recovering. Its hands twitched. Its posture straightened. Elias reached out. His fingers brushed the spiral etched into the alloy door.

At first, nothing. Then a pulse. Warmth spread through his hand. The metal vibrated soft at first, then deep. Symbols flared along the door like veins of light.

The Echo roared behind them. The door cracked open.

"Move!" Liora shouted.

They slipped through just as the destabilizer's field shattered and the Echo lunged. The door slammed shut behind them with a thunderous clang. Darkness swallowed them.

The room beyond was spherical walls etched with spirals and unfamiliar glyphs. The air was cooler here, but thick with static. At the center hovered a glassy column filled with drifting particles of light, like suspended stars.

Liora exhaled. "We made it."

Elias stared at the column. "Where are we?"

"An archive node," she said. "Hidden deep beneath the city. One of the oldest Lucid left it behind. We think it was a safe point. A place the system couldn't reach."

He moved closer, mesmerized by the light. As he approached, the particles responded spinning faster, orbiting around his presence. Liora watched with narrowed eyes.

"This place... it recognizes you," she said softly.

Elias looked back at her. "Why?"

"I don't know." She stepped beside him. "But if that Echo was chasing you, it means the Architects think you matter."

He stared at the lights again, voice low. "Then what am I supposed to do?"

"You survive," she said. "You learn. And when the time comes you resist."

They both looked back toward the sealed door. The Echo was still out there. Waiting.

Elias stood in the center of the archive chamber, surrounded by quiet light. It felt like standing inside a thought waiting to be remembered. The suspended particles shimmered like fireflies frozen in time. They moved when he breathed. Swirled when he stepped forward. Responded not mechanically, but *consciously*. Like they recognized something in him that even he didn't yet understand.

He felt Liora's eyes on him. "What is this place really?" he asked.

"Memory," she said. "Not yours. Not mine. But something older. From before the simulations hardened."

He turned to her. "Why show me this now?"

"Because you need to see the kind of world that's possible," she said.

A pulse echoed from the column. Then, a voice not external, but inside Elias's head. Gentle. Genderless.

"*You are not alone.*"

Elias flinched. "Did you hear that?"

Liora shook her head. "Hear what?"

He stepped back. The lights slowed their motion again.

"It said I'm not alone," he repeated.

"Good," Liora said. "You aren't."

She walked to a panel set into the wall, brushed away a layer of dust, and activated it. A small display flickered to life, cycling through corrupted data logs. Some were unreadable. Others contained images of faces half-rendered, coordinates blinking, and messages that ended mid-sentence. But one stood out. A single symbol. The spiral, once again. Only this time, the break through its center branched splitting into two directions. A choice.

Liora stared. "I've never seen that variant before."

Elias reached for it. The display shimmered.

A map bloomed across the room projected from the core. It displayed an aerial view of the city, but distorted. Fractured zones pulsed in gold, scattered across different sectors. Some blinked. Some remained still. One deep beneath the industrial block glowed brighter than the rest.

"What is that?" Elias asked.

Liora moved closer. "A signal."

"Is that where the breach is?" he asked.

"No." She looked troubled. "That might be something else entirely."

The lights dimmed. The map folded into a spiral. And a final phrase echoed through the chamber not from a speaker, not from the system. From the room itself.

"*The breach is not a door. It is a mirror.*"

The light collapsed. The column darkened. Elias stepped back, chilled. Liora powered down the terminal. "We've learned enough. For now."

They sat in silence for a long moment, catching their breath, letting their pulses slow. Then Elias spoke, voice softer than before. "What happens next?"

Liora looked at him with something between pride and caution. "We stop running. And we start choosing."

She stood, and offered him her hand. He took it.

The spiral marked the wall behind them. Glowing faintly. Waiting. As if it knew what came next.

CHAPTER SEVEN: BREADCRUMBS

The echo of their hurried footsteps faded into the dim, narrow hallway. The sound of survival was loud at the moment, yet vanishing too quickly to feel real. The door had hardly closed when exhaustion washed over Elias. His breath came in shallow, quick gasps, and his heart pounded from the near escape. However, the relief of safety didn't last. The walls felt too close, and the air was thick with the tension of what was coming next. This wasn't over—not by a long shot.

The hallway was dimly lit by flickering overhead bulbs that cast warped shadows along the cracked concrete. The scent of rust, mildew, and burnt circuitry clung to every surface. Even the air tasted recycled—dry and metallic, tinged with something faintly chemical. A low hum reverberated through the structure, as if the building held its breath.

Liora stepped away from the door, breathing deeply as she keyed in a code to unlock a hidden passageway in the wall. "We're safe for now," she said quietly, keeping her eyes sharp and alert. "The enforcers will comb the area but never find us here. We've made sure of that."

Still, Elias noticed how her fingers hovered near the side of her jacket—close to whatever blade or signaling device she carried. Safety was never absolute, but it was not anymore.

The air in the hallway pressed in like static. It wasn't loud but charged. Elias found himself holding his breath for reasons he couldn't name; as if the walls were listening and the space was aware of them. Maybe it was. He nodded, still reeling from their near escape. He couldn't shake the thought of how easily they could have been caught—how fragile their resistance truly was.

"This place... this hideout," Elias said, glancing around. It felt both lived-in and abandoned at the same time. Graffiti covered parts of the wall—some simple tags, others cryptic equations, patterns, and spirals half-scratched off. He knelt beside one that appeared fresh, the edges sharp and blackened as if it had been burned into the stone. He traced it with a finger, and the tip of his skin tingled for a moment.

"We don't draw them," Liora said from behind him. "They appear, usually when a fracture deepens. Like memories, the wall couldn't forget."

Elias stood slowly. "So this place... it's active."

She nodded. "Very."

The space was tight, the halls narrow, and the rooms makeshift. But the air felt dense—heavy with history and purpose. It wasn't the romanticized rebel base of legend but raw and real. "How long has this been here?"

"A long time," Liora replied, moving briskly toward a cluttered table in the corner. Maps, drives, documents—and computer terminals, some ancient and others strangely modern. She powered them up, her fingers flying with practiced speed. "This is where we analyze glitches, track system patterns, and pinpoint weaknesses." Elias stepped closer to the terminals. One of the screens was cycling through a series of fragmented video feeds—blurry loops lasting no longer than a second or two. Faces, walls, and symbols flickered out of sync.

"Are these from surveillance?" he asked.

Liora didn't look up. "Some of them. Others were smuggled out by people who didn't make it. We don't always know what they saw—just that they thought it mattered."

One video loop caught his eye: it showed a familiar corridor. A flash of a figure sprinted out of frame. The timestamp indicated it was dated two years ago, but the figure looked exactly like him. His gut twisted. It wasn't just a recording; it felt like a warning or a memory that hadn't happened yet.

"It's one of several safe houses hidden across the city. The resistance is small, but it's growing," she said.

As the room brightened from the screen's glow, Elias noticed scribbles along the walls—cryptic symbols, lines of code, and even poetry that seemed fragmented from half-erased minds. The symbols were familiar, remnants of the Lucid language his mother had shown him. He hovered over the maps covered in red marks—circles, crosses, and jagged notations. At first, they seemed like random data points, but the longer he stared, the more he saw patterns: fractal shapes and familiar paths. The chaos held structure.

"What are these coordinates?" he asked, curiosity creeping into his voice.

Liora paused before replying, her tone grave. "They're fracture zones—hotspots where resets tend to occur, where the system is most unstable. The fracture collapses from these points outward. If we can understand why, we might be able to break it."

Elias leaned closer. The maps were no longer abstract; they were blueprints of vulnerability. "So these are fault lines."

"Exactly. The system's weak spots."

Devin muttered from across the room, "It's evolving faster than we thought. This sector used to be quiet for weeks."

Camra scowled. "Because someone's leaking our movements." The tension in the room spiked. As they studied the data, Liora's breath caught. Her eyes locked onto a symbol pulsing on the screen—an anomaly. "This isn't right," she whispered, typing rapidly. "It's new. The system is responding faster than expected."

"What is it?" Elias asked.

"A breach. They've located this safe house. They're trying to destabilize the space around it."

Elias felt a chill. "So, we're compromised."

"We're out of time," Liora confirmed. She stood swiftly. "Pack everything you can carry. We move now." The room burst into motion. Satchels filled with drives, maps, and notes. Camra yanked power cells from their sockets while Devin grabbed a modular weapon from the wall.

Elias followed Liora's swift efficiency as she moved through the chaos, calm despite the urgency. She grabbed Taron's journal from a shelf, its edges worn and pages brittle. As she slid it into her coat, she recalled her brother's voice echoing in that last vision: "The symbols lead deeper."

"Our next safe house is further into the abandoned sectors. It's less fractured—for now. It'll buy us time," she said.

As they slipped into the city's shadows, Elias couldn't shake the feeling of being watched. Every flicker of light and every shifting shadow put him on edge. The city felt alive—metal grates rattled underfoot, hollow wind whispered through broken glass, and distant sirens seemed to echo from nowhere.

Stillness settled over them as they moved. Elias glanced at Liora, whose expression had hardened—her jaw tight, her eyes constantly scanning. Despite her steady composure, a flicker of weariness crossed her face. He stepped closer.

"You alright?" he asked.

She hesitated. "I'm used to running. I'm not used to watching it all unravel this fast."

Their eyes met. The tactical silence gave way to something more human—shared vulnerability and quiet trust.

"We'll make it," Elias said, surprising himself. "We have to."

Liora's smile was faint, almost invisible. "That's what my brother used to say."

They pressed onward through twisting alleys, past mural-covered walls glitching at the edges—visual artifacts of the fracture attempting to overwrite reality. A streetlamp flickered and briefly duplicated itself, casting two shadows where there should have been one. Elias shivered.

"This is deeper than I thought," Liora muttered, returning her gaze to the scanner. "They're not just reacting. They're anticipating."

Elias blinked. "What do you mean?"

"They're predicting our moves," she said, eyes locked on the readout. "The traps, the breaches—none of it is random. Someone is feeding them intel. Someone inside."

Elias's stomach turned. "A traitor?"

Liora didn't answer immediately. She nodded once, grimly. "We have a leak."

Elias's gaze snapped to each of them—Camra's silence, Devin's frown, Ashen's steady stare. Trust cracked like a fault line under his feet. As the team moved in tense silence, Elias studied their companions. Who among them had betrayed the resistance? Who was guiding the enforcers' hand?

They reached a temporary shelter inside the hollowed carcass of a transit hub—turnstiles rusted over, vending bots flickering in infinite error loops. There, they regrouped. Ashen lit a lantern, its faint orange glow barely pushing back the darkness.

Camra was the first to speak up: "We should vote. Everyone gets scanned. No exceptions."

Devin scoffed. "And if the spy is clever enough to mask their signature?"

Elias turned to Liora. "How do we find them?"

"We don't look for a person," Kyra explained. "We look for their method—how they're transmitting. If we track the signal, we track the spy."

Suddenly, her screen lit up—an alert, rapidly shifting coordinates pulsing like a beacon. "What is that?" Elias asked.

"A trap," Liora answered. "They're not waiting for us to act—they're setting the board. They already know where we're going."

Elias's mind reeled. The system wasn't just reacting; it was hunting. The Architects weren't merely watching anymore; they were controlling the game.

"Where do we go now?" he asked.

"There's one last safe house," she replied. "It's off-grid. If we can make it there, we can regroup and find the traitor."

As they slipped deeper into the city's underbelly, past relics of a world that had been rewritten too many times, Elias realized that the resistance wasn't just fighting a system anymore. They were contending with someone from within, and the betrayal had just begun. Somewhere in the system, something was watching—not for failure, but for deviation.

A faint memory stirred in Elias's mind—a voice, perhaps his mother's, warning him about the nature of the fractures.

"They're not random," she had said. "They're corrections." The system, whatever it was, didn't want to destroy; it tried to perfect it. It aimed to erase anomalies and rewrite what didn't fit its parameters.

As they navigated through the labyrinthine backstreets, Elias noticed strange architectural distortions—walls that seemed to breathe, doorways that didn't reasonably lead where they appeared to be. Reality itself was becoming unstable.

"The fracture's getting worse," Liora said, noticing his gaze. "Areas near the fault lines are the most vulnerable. Eventually, they'll be completely rewritten."

"And the people inside them?" Elias asked, already knowing the answer.

"Either absorbed into the new narrative or erased entirely," she replied. "Those who resist the changes become glitches themselves—scrambled, corrupted, and eventually degraded beyond recognition."

Suddenly, Devin raised a hand, signaling for them to stop. Ahead, the alley bent sharply around a corner, and he crept forward to check the path. After a tense moment, he waved them forward.

"Clear," he whispered, "but there's something you should see."

Around the bend, sprawled across an entire building facade, was a massive symbol—the same spiral pattern Elias had traced with his finger back at the hideout, but now enormous, glowing with a faint blue luminescence. Parts of it shifted subtly, like a hologram with unstable power.

"It's a beacon," Liora breathed. "A warning."

Ashen stepped closer, his young face reflecting the eerie blue light. "Or an invitation."

Camra grabbed his shoulder, pulling him back. "Don't get too close. Those who stare too long at the fractals start to fracture themselves."

But Elias couldn't look away. He began to see sequences within the spiraling patterns—not random, but precise. Mathematical. A language of sorts, speaking in geometric certainties. Somehow, deep in his core, he understood fragments of it.

"We need to document this," he said, reaching for his device. "It's not just warning us about the fractures—it's showing us their pattern, their progression."

Liora studied him with newfound intensity. "How do you know that?"

Elias hesitated. "I... I don't know. It's like I've seen this before." The admission hung between them, dangerous and revealing.

"Impossible," Kyra muttered. "Unless you've been closer to the center than anyone's ever gone."

The implication was clear—either Elias knew more than he was letting on, or something within him resonated with the system in ways they'd never seen before. Either way, he had made himself the most valuable or dangerous person in their group. Liora tensed her fingers on the scanner. "We should keep moving. The enforcers will have triangulated that beacon by now."

As they continued through the night, the abandoned sectors of the city gave way to stranger landscapes—half-formed buildings that seemed to phase in and out of existence, streets that looped back on themselves despite appearing straight. The fractures, in reality, were becoming worse, like fabric stretched to the breaking point.

"How much further?" Elias asked, his voice barely above a

whisper.

"Not far," Liora replied. "The next safe house is beneath the old data archives—a place so corrupted that even the system avoids it."

Devin snorted. "Great. So either we avoid detection, or we get scrambled trying."

"Better scrambled than reset," Ashen said quietly.

As they approached the archives—a massive, brutalist structure half-collapsed into itself—Elias felt a strange pull, as if gravity were shifting beneath his feet. The building seemed to bend toward him, as though recognizing something in his presence.

"Do you feel that?" he asked.

The others shook their heads, but Liora observed him. "What is it?"

"It's like... it knows me," he replied.

Before she could respond, a piercing alarm cut through the night—high and thin, almost beyond human hearing. Camra clutched her head, her data port suddenly flashing red.

"Breach!" she gasped. "They've found us. The signal—it's coming from—"

Her words were cut off as she stared at Elias, horror dawning on her face.

"It's you," she whispered. "You're the beacon."

CHAPTER EIGHT: FALSE WAKE

The flickering overhead lights were the first sign that something was wrong. Elias stood in the corner of the dim room, watching as the others gathered around the central table, their faces illuminated by the sickly blue glow of the monitors. His shoulders tensed beneath his worn leather jacket, and his fingers tapped restlessly against his thigh in an unconscious rhythm that matched his racing heartbeat.

Liora had been quiet for hours, studying the data on the screens. Her dark eyes were narrowed as she muttered to herself, fingers flying across the keyboard with practiced precision. The soft clicking sounds created an anxious soundtrack to their waiting.

The tension in the air was palpable—an electric undercurrent that was impossible to ignore, like the charged atmosphere before a devastating storm. The walls of their hideout, a converted warehouse in the forgotten district, seemed to have thickened overnight, pressing inward with the weight of unseen forces, constricting around them like a slowly tightening fist. Reality itself felt braced for impact as if the molecules were vibrating with anticipation of the coming disruption.

Beyond the walls, the city had descended into an unnatural silence. A hush hung in the air like a funeral shroud, smothering the usual cacophony of urban life: the constant hum of vehicles, the distant wail of sirens, and the murmur of countless voices blending into white noise. Light filtered through the boarded windows, appearing distorted, stretched thin, and gray, as though some unseen force manipulated the very wavelengths. Even the familiar metallic groans of the city's aging infrastructure had faded, replaced by an ominous stillness—the kind that precedes catastrophe, causing prey animals to freeze in their tracks, sensing a predator's approach.

Elias moved to the wall, pressing his palm against the cool concrete. The surface vibrated not with sound but tension, like a violin string pulled too tight. He closed his eyes and sensed a shift somewhere deep below. It wasn't a physical change but a cognitive one, as if the system had blinked, rewriting something fundamental, forgetting and remembering simultaneously. Whatever had changed, it was significant.

"Something's happening," Elias said, his voice barely above a whisper. The hairs on his neck stood on end, instincts screaming danger. Liora didn't respond immediately, absorbed in the data before her, but eventually paused to meet his gaze, her brow furrowing. She powered down the monitor with a deliberate gesture. "You feel it too, don't you?" she asked, her voice steady despite the weight of her words.

"It's like the rules are different today," Elias said, rubbing his temple. "It feels like gravity has shifted."

Liora nodded slowly, rising from her chair. "We call it a pulse. It's like the system's heart skipping a beat and then rewriting its rhythm. This usually happens during a small reset—protocols, zoning, crowd logic."

"But this isn't small," he said, swallowing hard.

"No," she agreed, her eyes darkening. "This is defensive,

which means we've triggered something real."

Elias nodded, scanning the room. It wasn't just the flickering lights or eerie silence; it was that crawling sensation of being watched. That feeling had always lurked beneath the surface, but today, it felt closer—more invasive. The other Lucid individuals looked up, their expressions mirroring his unease. Camra stood by the far wall, arms tightly folded across her chest, fingers digging into her biceps, while Devin loaded a weapon with slow, deliberate motions that revealed his anxiety.

"They've cut communications in Grid Seven," Camra announced, her voice taut as a wire. "All Lucid activity went dark twenty minutes ago. No signals. No residuals."

"That's not suppression," Liora said quietly, exchanging a meaningful glance with Elias. "That's erasure."

Ashen halted his restless pacing. "Do you think they triggered a full protocol?" Liora's silence answered more eloquently than words.

Ashen resumed pacing, muttering curses under his breath. Everyone in the resistance had sensed the shift—a faint signal that the system was reacting to their presence, adapting to hunt them.

"We're being tracked," Liora concluded, leaning over the holographic map and tracing a pattern only she could see. "The system has learned how to detect us. It's been adapting faster than we anticipated. They're coming for us."

Before Elias could respond, the door to their hideout crashed open with a thunderous impact. The sound reverberated through the room, sending adrenaline surging through his veins. Several Lucid members leaped to their feet, faces draining of color, but Liora raised a steady hand.

"Stay calm," she commanded, her voice sharp but controlled.

"This isn't a random raid. They've located us specifically. The enforcers are close."

Elias's heart hammered against his ribs as he backed toward the corner, fighting to control his breathing. The enforcers were coming; it had only been a matter of time before the system found them and before they faced erasure, wiped from existence as thoroughly as deleted files. Camra checked the battery levels of two hand-assembled EMP charges and then glanced toward Liora. "Ready when you are."

"Cover the rear exit," Liora instructed, slipping a compact device into her pocket. "If they breach both entrances, we'll funnel them into the middle."

"Won't that trap us too?" Devin questioned, his voice low but firm, hand tightening around his weapon.

"Only if we wait too long," Liora replied, the ghost of a smile touching her lips.

Elias pressed against the wall, struggling to steady his breathing. The walls around him seemed to shift subtly, triggering a buried memory—a childhood fragment from before he awakened and became Lucid.

He was seven, playing with a small metallic puzzle cube in the living sector. His mother smiled from across the table, sunlight catching in her hair. Then, without warning, everything paused. Colors drained from the world, voices silenced mid-sentence. A white light consumed everything; when it receded, his mother was gone. A different woman stood in her place. She smiled, but not like his mother had. It was the first reset he remembered and the last he dared mention. He had tried once, and the silence that followed had been deafening.

He snapped back to the present as Ashen approached, tension evident in every line of his body. "You ever think we're chasing ghosts?" Ashen asked, his eyes darting toward the door.

Elias gave him a sidelong glance. "What do you mean?"

Ashen shrugged, fingers drumming against his thigh. "Even if we win... do we get it back? Our lives, our memories? Or just another version of ourselves who'll get wiped, too?"

Before Elias could answer, the floor beneath them shuddered violently.

The resistance members scrambled, gathering weapons and positioning themselves strategically. Elias's thoughts raced, but one certainty remained: they couldn't let the enforcers capture them. They couldn't afford to be reset. Not now. Not when they were so close to uncovering the truth.

Suddenly, the door exploded inward. The enforcers flooded into the room—black-clad figures moving with inhuman precision. Their emotionless efficiency sent ice through Elias's veins. Faces were hidden behind obsidian helmets; expressions were nonexistent; they didn't need expressions. They were programmed for a single purpose: hunt and destroy. The room erupted into chaos.

The first EMP detonated like a silent tsunami; lights surged and died. In the strobing emergency LEDs, Elias glimpsed at Liora, dragging an injured Camra away from the console. At the same time, Devin fired bursts from a pulse rifle, each shot illuminating the scene in stark relief.

Liora was the first to react decisively. She grabbed Elias's arm with an iron grip, yanking him toward a narrow hallway at the back of the room. "Everyone, go!" she shouted, her voice cutting through the chaos. "Get to the safe house!"

Elias hesitated, watching as Devin was surrounded, but the determination blazing in Liora's eyes brooked no argument. There was no time. He turned and sprinted down the hallway, lungs burning as he pushed himself to the limit. Behind him, the cacophony intensified: shouting, the clash of weapons, the mechanical growls of the enforcers. But he couldn't stop. Survival demanded forward motion.

As he neared the exit, a scream pierced the chaos—not just any scream, but one that belonged to their own. It wasn't just any scream. It was Kyra. Elias spun toward the sound, the room flickering in and out of focus like a dying transmission. He found her near the broken monitors, half-shadowed, half-light. An Enforcer grabbed her wrist, raising a silver device to her temple. Kyra jerked away, but reality itself betrayed her—the air around her rippling, folding. She glitched.

Her outline stuttered, fragmenting into flickering copies: one reaching out, one gasping, one already falling away. The copies overlapped, blurred, and dissolved. She wasn't being dragged. She was being rewritten.

Kyra locked eyes with Elias across the battlefield of collapsing light. Her mouth moved, soundless—a whisper swallowed by the system.

Remember.

Then her body unraveled into static, pixel by pixel, as if the world had decided she was never there at all. First her hands, then her arms, then her wide, furious eyes.

In her place, the concrete wall stood unbroken, seamless.

As if she'd always been part of it.

A faint spiral glowed for a heartbeat on the floor where she had been—a brand, a signature, or maybe a promise.

Elias staggered back, choking on air that felt thinner, wrong. He wanted to scream, to tear open the world with his bare hands, but instinct roared louder: move.

He turned and ran, Kyra's vanishing burning into the backs

of his eyes.

Elias froze, blood turning to ice in his veins. His eyes locked with Liora's for a heartbeat, long enough to witness the raw terror distorting her features. "Go!" she commanded, desperation edging her voice. "Elias, go!"

The enforcers had taken one of them. The scream wasn't merely one of pain; it was the sound of someone being reset. Erased. His chest constricted, panic threatening to overwhelm him, but he forced himself to move forward. The resistance was fracturing before his eyes. They were being hunted, and their safe spaces were compromised individually.

Elias burst through the exit just as another wave of enforcers flooded the hallway. He didn't look back; he couldn't afford to. He plunged into the darkness, breath ragged as he navigated the labyrinthine streets. The world blurred around him—shadowed alleys, abandoned storefronts—his heartbeat thundering in his ears. He had no destination beyond escape, beyond survival. The sounds of pursuit gradually faded, but he knew better than to slow down. Enforcers never stopped.

As he raced past shattered windows and fractured façades, the city's distortions became increasingly apparent. Streetlights stuttered, and buildings blurred at their edges, trembling between states of existence. A massive billboard cycled through the same commercial loop until it glitched, displaying Elias's expressionless face for a half-second—a version of himself already rewritten, staring back with empty eyes. Then static consumed the image.

Rounding a corner, his hope evaporated. There was nowhere left to run. The streets had emptied, footsteps echoing from every direction. The enforcers had outmaneuvered him, closing in on their trap. He turned to face them, chest heaving. Their blank helmets reflected his fear back at him as they advanced. They weren't there to capture him; they had come to reset him. To erase his existence entirely.

Just as he braced for the inevitable, a voice called from the shadows.

"Elias!"

He spun around, heart leaping. There, in the darkness of the alley, stood Liora. Alone but undaunted, determination burning in her eyes. She hadn't abandoned him. She had come back.

"They're almost here," she warned, breathless. "We need to go. Now!"

Elias didn't hesitate. Together, they sprinted down the alley, the enforcers' mechanized footsteps echoing behind them. The safe house lay just ahead—a sanctuary within reach. But Elias faltered as they approached the door, a terrible realization surfacing.

"They're resetting people," he said, his voice breaking. "Erasing us. Trying to stop us. But what happens to them? To the ones who get erased?"

Liora's expression tightened, sorrow mingling with resolve. "They forget," she said softly. "They lose everything: memories, past, identity—their existence. It's like they never were. They're just... gone. And the system continues, unaltered and unchallenged."

Elias felt a tight knot in his stomach. The reset wasn't just a weapon but the ultimate tool for control and erasure. It was worse than death; it meant the obliteration of ever having lived at all. Suddenly, Camra's voice crackled through Liora's wrist communicator: "Two minutes, max. Then we're ghosts. Get inside."

In the darkness, Elias's eyes adjusted enough to make out a glyph burned into the doorframe—an ancient Lucid symbol, partially scorched but still visible. It pulsed faintly, a beacon of defiance. They hadn't lost—not yet. But the system was rewriting reality faster than they could resist its changes.

CHAPTER NINE: HIDDEN HISTORIES

The path to Subsector 19 was not marked on any current system, at least not officially. It was a myth among the Lucid—a whispered echo passed through back-alley glyphs and fragmented dream-logs. Yet as Elias moved through the abandoned tunnels, he kept thinking he saw her—Kyra—just ahead. A flicker of dark hair, a shape slipping around a corner, always vanishing before he could call out. His chest tightened. He hadn't saved her. He hadn't even tried. He'd frozen when she needed him most, while the system unmade her before his eyes.He shoved the guilt down deep, but it clung to him like static, whispering in the empty air.

Elias felt a pull toward it now—like gravity or instinct as if it were something left behind for him to discover. The signal shard in his pocket vibrated gently but insistently, like a compass needle quivering in the presence of something buried.

He checked his surroundings. The corridor was empty, devoid of shadows or enforcers. Elias ducked beneath a half-collapsed archway, the steel above him etched with marks that resembled claw swipes. Half-erased spiral graffiti stretched along the length of the wall. A rusted sign read: MAINTENANCE—TIER C (DEPRECATED). He pressed onward, his boots echoing with hollow thuds against the forgotten concrete.

The city's usual hum—factory pistons, announcements, synchronized footfalls—was absent here. Instead, a strange sound filled the void: subtle static, a whisper that seemed to ride the air. It felt less like sound and more like presence, a memory struggling to be born. Elias descended deeper into the dark and eventually reached the threshold.

Before him stood a wide, sealed door. Unlike the sterilized surfaces above, this one was scorched and battered. Weld marks lined its edges, indicating that someone had attempted to lock it permanently while another had tried even harder to pry it open. In the center, a faded spiral was drawn in charcoal black, surrounded by a crude glyph. He reached forward, brushing his fingers against the spiral. The metal pulsed under his touch. With a shudder, the door slid open. The air inside was still—not dead, but waiting.

The room was massive and dome-like, constructed with an older architectural style. Elias stepped into a space that resembled a fusion of an archive, command center, and tomb. Terminals lined the perimeter, their displays either dark or blinking faintly with error codes. Old chairs were either over-turned or buried beneath yellowing folders. Dozens of sheets of real paper were scattered across metal desks: drawings, maps, schematics, and journal entries, all centered around a single motif: the spiral.

At the center of the chamber was a mural that stretched across nearly the entire far wall. Elias stared breath caught in his throat. It was her—his mother. The image was stylized, painted in broad, impressionistic strokes, yet unmistakable. Her face appeared fierce yet kind, her hands held open, and her eyes were wide with something like sorrow. Behind her, the spiral bloomed outward like wings. Beneath the mural was a plaque that read, "The erased do not disappear. They persist in echo."

Elias stepped forward, the air feeling heavy as if the cathedral held its breath. The closer he moved, the more the room shimmered at the edges. The lights overhead flickered in a rhythm he had begun to recognize—a pattern: 3-2-3. It was the same one she used to hum when he was a child. He reached a trembling hand toward the painting.

"Stop right there," a voice said behind him, calm and tired yet familiar. Elias spun around. Harlen stood in the doorway, arms folded across his chest.

"You found it," Harlen said, stepping further into the archive and scanning the mural as if he hadn't seen it in years. "We built this place in fragments—salvaged parts and partial memories. Your mother started with dreams. I filled in the wiring."

"You knew this was here?" Elias asked.

"I helped build it," Harlen replied. "Back when your mother was still alive. Back before the first reset."

Elias narrowed his eyes. "Reset?"

Harlen sat heavily on an old stool, wiping dust from his palms. "The system resets reality when it senses instability—memories, people, language—rewritten from top to core." He pointed upward. "Every fracture we map risks another purge. That's why this place is off the grid."

"She was part of this?" Elias asked, stepping closer to the mural.

"She led it," Harlen said. "Your mother was one of the earliest Lucids. She didn't just see the cracks; she walked through them." Elias felt the floor shift under the weight of that truth. He glanced again at the painted spiral blooming behind her. "Why didn't anyone tell me? Why did everyone pretend she was just—gone?"

Harlen's jaw clenched. "Because that's what the Architects want. Forgetting is easier than questioning. They don't just erase people; they erase the memory of memory." A beat of silence passed.

"I always remembered her humming," Elias whispered. "Even after she vanished. That pattern is 3-2-3. It never left me."

Harlen smiled faintly. "That's not a lullaby; that's a breach code."

Elias blinked. "What?"

Harlen stood and moved to one of the functioning terminals. He typed in a sequence, and the screen glowed blue, flickering with static before resolving into a series of interconnected spirals mapped across a grid of city districts. "Every time someone resists—truly resists—it leaves a mark: a breach. And those breaches connect, forming something bigger than even the Architects understand." The map zoomed in on a cluster labeled ECHO_72. One of the spirals glowed brighter than the others.

"This is where you are now," Harlen said. "This archive isn't just a memory vault; it's a convergence point."

Elias stepped away from the mural, overwhelmed. "How many people remember this place?"

Harlen's face darkened. "Not many. We've lost most of them over the resets. Some vanished; some... changed."

"Changed?" Elias asked.

"They stopped being themselves," Harlen replied. "You can watch someone's soul get rewritten in real-time. They start forgetting names, faces, then entire years. And then, one day, they're quoting system doctrine as if they were born to it." Elias felt his stomach twist.

"That's what's waiting for all of us," Harlen said. "Unless we find the Core."

Elias turned sharply. "You mean Liora's Core?"

Harlen nodded. "If we find it, we find the heart of the simulation. We find the fracture that can't be patched."

Elias's mind buzzed. It felt like too much—too many truths at once.

"I need to know more," he said. "About my mother. About what she did here."

Harlen hesitated, then moved to a locked cabinet and retrieved a small metal case. Inside was a datapad wrapped in cloth, with a spiral carved into its back.

"She left this for you," Harlen said. "She told me to hold onto it until you found your way here." Elias reached for it with shaking hands. The screen lit up before he touched it. The datapad blinked awake. Elias held his breath as the screen dissolved into a static field, then resolved into a glowing spiral that pulsed slowly with each heartbeat. It was subtle, yet alive. The image shimmered, and a recording began to play. Not a video, but a voice.

"Elias... if you're hearing this, you've found what I couldn't finish." His mother's voice.

Younger than he remembered, stronger, too. Clearer than his memories had ever rendered her.

"They'll tell you I left, that I gave up, that I was unstable. None of it is true. I left to protect you, to leave something behind—something they couldn't rewrite." Elias's throat tightened. "I've seen the breach with my own eyes. I've stepped into the memory behind the lie. I've felt the world unwrite itself around me. But the truth holds. Even now, even here. You are part of it. You always have been." The recording ended. No signature, no farewell. Just a soft chime, and then the spiral faded. Elias lowered the pad, his eyes stinging. "She knew," he said. "She knew I'd end up here."

Harlen nodded, his voice gentler now. "Your mother was like you. She remembered things no one else could. She used to say the spiral wasn't just a symbol but a shape language. A memory engine." He turned to a corner of the room and pulled back a curtain of cables, revealing a worn wall etched with crude, colorful chalk marks—circles, spirals, arrows. Words scratched into a child's hand. "Ilya," Harlen said. "My daughter."

Elias approached the wall slowly. She had written in overlapping layers as if she had kept returning, trying to remember what she once knew. At the center was a phrase in bold red crayon:

"THEY ARE MAKING US FORGET."

Beneath it:

"THEY DON'T DREAM."

And finally:

"REMEMBER HER."

Elias traced the last line with his fingers. "She remembered your daughter," he said quietly. "They remembered each other." Harlen stepped back as if the words had struck him in the chest. He was silent for a moment.

"She used to say the walls were listening," he murmured. "Not out of fear, just... like she wanted to say something back."

Elias studied the layers, trying to piece together the girl's thoughts. A map of symbols began to take shape. They weren't random; they spiraled inward, pointing to a specific mark on the grid—one of the breach marks Harlen had shown him. "You said these are still active?" Elias asked.

Harlen nodded. "The deeper the memory, the harder it is for the Architects to erase. Some places—especially those with strong emotional signatures—remain fractured longer."

Elias turned, urgency blooming in his chest. "Then we need to go there," he said. "Now."

Harlen blinked. "It's not that simple."

"Why not?" Elias asked irritably.

"Because getting near a breach affects you," Harlen explained. "Time warps. Identity bleeds. The last Lucid who made direct contact didn't return the same."

Elias met his gaze. "But they came back."

Harlen was quiet for a moment. Then he said, "Some part of them did."

They moved quickly. Harlen handed him a battered satchel filled with tools—a signal lens, a spiral reader, and a disruptor pen. "Don't trust anything you see inside the breach," Harlen warned. "Not even yourself."

Elias paused at the door. "Why now?" he asked. "Why show me all this?"

"Because you're ready," Harlen said. "And because the spiral's moving again."

Elias stepped into the corridor, his pulse quickening with each footfall. The datapad buzzed faintly at his side, illuminating a path toward the breach site. It led him not to the city's edges but deeper—into the heart of the system, toward a place known in Lucid code as THREADPOINT ZERO. The stairwell was narrow, lit only by flickering backup lights. A nearby vent hissed constantly, leaking warm air with a static charge. As he descended, Elias began to notice things shifting again. The walls shimmered when he wasn't looking directly at them. Out of the corner of his eye, symbols flickered on the surface and then vanished.

The spiral.

The hallway opened into a chamber that looked... wrong. It resembled a maintenance room, but the materials were all out of place. The walls pulsed softly, almost like a muscle. The overhead pipes bent into curves that matched the spiral pattern. The air shimmered with potential. In the center of the room floated a distortion—visible only through the signal lens. It appeared as a faint ripple in the shape of a teardrop. Reality bent inward around it. The datapad lit up: BREACH IDENTIFIED. THREADPOINT ZERO. Elias stepped closer, and the distortion pulsed.

For a split second, his vision narrowed, and he saw—a memory. Not his. A girl—with dark hair and bare feet hummed as she ran her fingers along a wall. Ilya. She turned and smiled—not at him, but past him. For a moment, he wondered if she saw someone else, too. Maybe Taron. Maybe someone is still trapped inside. Then, her image shattered into pixels and vanished. Another vision replaced it: his mother, seated beside a glowing shard. Her voice whispered something he couldn't hear. The words dissolved before they reached him. He stepped into the breach. The world inverted. Not visually—existentially. Elias felt himself lifted and folded as if his consciousness were a page being turned. Sound collapsed. Color burned inward. Time hiccuped.

When the world righted itself, he stood in a place he didn't recognize—but somehow remembered. A courtyard of black grass lay beneath a pale orange sky, with monolithic towers rising like fingers from the ground. At the center, a pool of still water shaped the spiral itself. He stepped forward. His reflection in the water wasn't his own. The man who stared back was older, worn, with eyes lit by golden static. The reflection spoke.

"You're not the first. But you might be the last."

Elias staggered back. "What is this?"

"This is what they tried to burn. But it remembers." The reflection began to shimmer, breaking apart into fragments. Each fragment showed a face—his mother, Harlen's daughter, Liora, and others he didn't recognize. The spiral bound them all.

Then, a harsh and digital siren screamed in the distance. The simulation was collapsing. Elias ran. When he burst out of the chamber and back into the hallway, the door behind him slammed shut. The breach was sealed with a crack like lightning and vanished. He stumbled forward, gasping. The datapad at his side now glowed bright gold. On the screen, a single phrase pulsed: THREADPOINT ZERO UNLOCKED.

Back at the Echo Archive, Harlen waited. Elias dropped the datapad on the desk.

"You went in?" Harlen asked, his eyes wide.

Elias nodded. "I saw her. Your daughter. I saw... everyone."

Harlen sat slowly, his gaze distant. "What did they say?" he asked.

"That I might be the last," Elias replied.

Harlen smiled a cracked and weary expression. "Then we'd better make it count." He tapped a panel, activating a terminal embedded in the floor. Elias looked at him. "What now?"

Harlen's eyes locked onto his. "We don't find the Core," he said. "We become it." A golden spiral flickered beneath the terminal's surface as he spoke—faint but pulsing in time with

Elias's breath. He wasn't walking away from the resistance—not really. He was stepping beyond the network they had built, chasing a piece of it none had reached. For now, that meant walking alone. But not without purpose.

CHAPTER TEN: SPARK OF DOUBT

Elias woke to a deep silence that felt like pressure—a weighted stillness that settled in his bones. He didn't know how long he had slept; his trusted clocks had stopped updating. Light leaked through the vents in amber streaks, casting the room in a false dawn. Maybe it was morning, or the system was simulating one for his benefit. The datapad beside his cot still glowed with a golden spiral, the word "UNLOCKED" pulsing like a heartbeat. He didn't touch it. Every time he did, something in the world shifted—barely perceptible but tangible. A corner would stretch too far, the lights would pulse in sync with his rhythm, or someone would look at him too long. Something was watching or perhaps echoing him.

Elias sat up slowly. The cot groaned under his weight, and his back cracked like glass. He hadn't eaten since the breach, and while food didn't feel necessary, he knew that wasn't normal. He was changing. Something had started inside him, and it was quietly completing its cycle.

He opened the hatch above the stairwell and climbed into the corridor. The world had changed again. The light in the tunnel was bluer than yesterday—not just filtered but saturated, like it was bleeding from the walls themselves. The air felt different, too—thicker. It dragged slightly when he moved through it, like walking underwater. He blinked rapidly and forced himself to move forward.

Aboveground, the city pulsed with activity, but everything felt wrong. The usual drone of synchronized movement was out of step. Workers walked, but their heads jerked subtly, like puppets on stiff strings. One woman across the platform froze mid-step, staring at nothing for nearly thirty seconds before moving again. No one reacted, not even a glance in her direction.

Elias pressed into the crowd, fighting the nausea rising in his chest. The whole city felt like it had been re-rendered slightly off-axis. Familiar buildings now had misplaced windows. Vendors he passed daily were gone, replaced by featureless blank booths. The smell of ozone had deepened, electric and sharp. Reality was rebalancing itself—correcting for what he had seen in the breach and, in some way, correcting him.

He walked until he found the spot—the bakery. It was still there, but it felt wrong, like the world had used a faulty backup file to rebuild it. It was almost right but soulless. The awning was pure white and blank, with no signage. The windows showed no pastries or warmth, just a clean, sterile interior that looked like a display model—never lived in. Yet the spiral had returned, etched into the glass from the inside.

Elias stepped closer, his hand out. His breath fogged the glass and distorted the symbol. In a flicker, for half a heartbeat, his reflection was not his own. It was different—older, with golden eyes. The expression was unreadable. He backed away quickly.

He turned into an alley near the old freight lines and followed a series of hand-scrawled glyphs that only Lucids would notice.

They led him to a locked service hatch in the old Echo network. The access pad buzzed as he held his shard near it, and it clicked open. The stairs spiraled down like everything else.

He found Harlen deep in the archive, hunched over a projector and rerouting signal maps. Elias didn't announce his presence, but Harlen sensed him anyway.

"You've been drifting," Harlen said.

"I haven't gone back to Threadpoint," Elias replied.

"I didn't say you had." Harlen turned, his face heavy with concern. The lines under his eyes had deepened. "You feel it too, don't you? The distortion."

Elias nodded. "I can't trust my memories anymore. Things I knew last week feel planted, like props in a dream I didn't agree to."

Harlen paused, then pulled a sheet of data film from a drawer and laid it on the light table. "This used to show three anchor points in District Seven," he said. "Last night, it showed six. This morning... it shows none." He flipped the film. "It's not glitching. The system is responding. It's trying to erase its own fractures before we reach them."

Elias stared in disbelief. "Then we're running out of time."

"No," Harlen corrected. "You are."

They moved into the back vault, where the resonance scanner was kept. Harlen activated it, aiming the cylindrical device at Elias's chest.

"What are you doing?" Elias asked, a note of apprehension in his voice.

"Testing something," Harlen replied. "Stand still."

The device whined softly before beeping. Harlen examined the readout, his brows furrowing in concern.

"What?" Elias pressed.

"You're broadcasting," Harlen said, his voice tense. "At a low frequency, but it's consistent. Rhythmic."

"Broadcasting what?"

"Signal code. Refracted memory." Harlen looked up, his expression grave. "You're leaking, Elias."

Elias suddenly felt cold, like something had been stripped away without permission. The datapad in his coat buzzed. He pulled it out to find the spiral had changed from gold to red. A single line of text scrolled beneath it: CORE ANOMALY DETECTED.

Harlen read it too, and his jaw tightened. "We have to move."

"To where?" Elias asked, panic rising in his chest.

"Wherever it leads," Harlen replied.

Elias stared at the screen in disbelief. "Liora's missing," he said. "I haven't seen her since I came back." Perhaps that was part of the design. Liora never vanished without a reason; she tested people, pushing them toward thresholds. This could be another threshold.

Harlen didn't meet his eyes. "She's always been on her own loop. We intersect when needed."

"That's not an answer," Elias snapped.

"No," Harlen admitted. "It's not."

Elias turned away, his head buzzing and his heart racing. "Who can I trust?" he asked finally.

Harlen didn't hesitate. "Only memory. Yours. Not mine. Not Liora's. Just what stays when the rest fades."

Elias nodded slowly, feeling the weight of that truth settle in his bones. He would follow the signal—not because Harlen said so, nor because Liora wanted him to, but because he needed to understand what had changed in him, what the system was trying to rewrite, and why, despite everything, it felt like someone inside him was whispering back.

The signal led Elias deeper into the old city, beyond mapped corridors and past where the spirals faded from the walls, into places where even memory hesitated. He didn't bring Harlen—not because he didn't trust him, but because he couldn't afford anyone else's fear.

Elias needed clarity, and lately, he felt like every conversation was being translated from a language that was no longer spoken. The datapad in his coat continued to pulse, growing brighter with each step. It no longer displayed text; instead, it showed an animated spiral, slowly rotating clockwise, pulling him along like gravity.

He stopped before a broken transit gate leading to a disused line: SECTOR 3-A, BLOCKED. The sign had flickered red for years, but now it blinked green. Elias stepped through.

The tunnel beyond was filled with silence—not the kind of emptiness that suppresses noise, but a silence that made his ears ring as if to remind him that sound used to exist.

He passed through a checkpoint with shattered glass and a control booth half-melted from some ancient system failure. Graffiti lined the walls—unlike the tight, coded spirals of Lucid messages, these were wilder, raw emotions scrawled in charcoal and dried paint:

"DO NOT TRUST HER."

"I MET MYSELF HERE. I DID NOT SURVIVE."

"THE CORE IS YOU. RUN."

Each message cut like a whisper from a life that no longer existed. The spiral on his datapad pulsed red, blue, and red. The breach was close.

He reached a chamber where the tunnel collapsed inward. In the void left by the damage, reality twisted. It was initially subtle—a shimmer of heat, a flicker of shadow moving the wrong way. Then it coalesced into something tangible: a ripple in the air, like a soap bubble in reverse. A pull. A new breach.

He stepped closer, not bothering with the lens this time. He could feel it. As he approached, the air thickened, and his limbs moved slower—not because of weight, but because time fought him here. Still, he reached out and touched the edge of the breach.

It swallowed him instantly.

He woke in a garden—not one he'd ever seen but one that felt familiar. The grass was black under his palms, the sky was silver overhead, and trees bent like question marks, their leaves vibrating gently in the breeze. The air smelled of citrus and static.

Elias stood slowly, his mind adapting to match the rhythm of this place. It was quiet but not dead. The silence here was thoughtful, almost watchful. At the center of the clearing stood a figure.

Liora. Or something that looked like her.

She wore no disguise or cloak—just a plain white shirt and bare feet. Her face was calm, her expression unreadable. Elias didn't speak; he didn't trust this.

She smiled. "You're not afraid of me."

"Not yet," he replied. "But I probably should be."

The smile remained. "You're different now. The breach didn't just touch you; it tethered to you."

Elias kept his distance. "Are you real?" The way she moved and spoke wasn't quite her, but it wasn't far off either. Perhaps Liora had left behind more than just words. Maybe this was part of her plan.

"I'm real enough," she said. "But that's not what you're

asking."

"No," Elias said. "I'm asking if you're here. The real Liora, or just a system copy meant to manipulate me."

She laughed—tired, not mocking. "Does it matter?"

"Yes," Elias said flatly.

The wind changed direction. Liora stepped closer. "If I said I was her," she said, "would you believe me?"

"No," he replied. "I've seen things that shouldn't be possible. My reflection isn't mine anymore. Buildings rearrange themselves when I walk past. The system is rewriting everything just to keep up with me."

"And yet," she said, "you still followed the spiral."

"Because I want answers."

Liora or her shade nodded. "You'll get one," she said. "But only one."

She reached behind her and pulled something from the air: a folded piece of black metal, smooth as glass and engraved with a spiral. She handed it to him. The moment he touched it, something unlocked in his mind—a memory that wasn't his.

He stood in a white room—clean, surgical, and empty except for a chair and a monitor. A younger version of himself sat in the chair—ten, maybe twelve years old. His mother stood behind him, her hands resting on his shoulders. The screen flashed images: faces, maps, codes, and the spiral.

"You're going to forget," she said gently.

"But I don't want to," young Elias replied.

"You have to. If you remember too soon, they'll find you. They'll take everything back." She leaned down, kissed his temple, and whispered, "The spiral will bring you back."

The vision shattered. Elias fell to his knees, gasping. Liora watched, patient. He looked up, his eyes wet. "That wasn't a memory. That was... a buried command."

"A truth," she said. "Locked away. Now retrieved."

He stood. "Why show me now?"

"Because you're ready to choose." She gestured around the garden. "This breach exists outside system control. For now. But not for long. When it collapses, you won't be able to return here again."

"What are my choices?" Elias asked desperately.

"You can go back to Echo. Let Harlen lead. Allow the spiral to continue slowly unraveling the city."

"And the other option?" Elias pleaded.

"Take what's changed inside you. Leave them all behind. Go deeper. Find the Core. Rewrite the ending yourself."

Elias remained silent for a long time. Finally, he asked, "If I choose the second option, do I ever return?"

"No," she said. "But you might be remembered."

The breach shimmered around them. The garden began to peel away, petals rising like paper torn in the wind. Time was running out.

Liora stepped toward him one last time. "Do you want to know if I'm her?" she asked.

He nodded.

"I don't know anymore," she said. "I remember being Liora. I remember the resistance, the messages. But I also remember dying." She touched his chest. "And I remember you."

He reached for her, but she was already vanishing. The world fractured.

He woke at the edge of the breach. His body ached, and his chest burned where she had touched him. He pulled off his coat. Something glowed beneath his skin. Lifting his shirt, he saw it—a spiral projected, not tattooed. It shimmered in pale blue light just beneath the surface of his skin, pulsing, alive.

It had embedded itself in him—not just symbolically, but literally. He stood alone in the tunnel. The datapad was dead. Harlen wouldn't find him. Echo was behind him now. There was no map of where he was going—only the spiral, the Echo, only memory.

He wasn't lost. He was following something no map could trace, carried forward by memory, design, and the Echo of others who had made it this far. If he saw them again, it would be as someone new.

He stepped forward into the dark.

CHAPTER ELEVEN: BREAKING THE SCRIPT

The city felt different now, though not in any obvious ways. The buildings remained the same, and the streets echoed with the sounds of machinery and the dull murmur of movement. Workers marched in cadence, and the system continued whispering soft, quiet commands. But Elias had changed, and now the city could no longer deceive him as it once had. He walked purposefully through the outer districts, where surveillance was sparser, and reality flickered more often. His body moved as if he belonged there, but inside, nothing felt right.

The spiral beneath his skin pulsed faintly with each step, recognizing the ground patterns and warning him about them. For three days since the breach, he had wandered the fractured seams of the grid, searching for something he couldn't yet name. He was following the spiral, listening to the hum beneath the streets, and waiting for the world to make a mistake he could slip through. He wasn't running from Harlen or Liora; he simply couldn't wait for them any longer.

This quest—whatever it was—belonged to him alone. On the fourth night, he found the door. It was hidden in plain sight, part of a delivery hub on the edge of the industrial ring.

Thousands of people passed it daily without a second glance, but it pulsed with energy tonight. Although the pulsing wasn't visibly mechanical, the air around it seemed to thrum in a rhythm: three short beats, two long, three short again. This pattern had haunted him for weeks.

Elias reached into his coat and pulled out his dead datapad, its black screen. However, when he raised it toward the door, the metal shimmered. He placed his palm flat against the center panel, and the door opened—no hiss, no welcome, just a heavy silence. He stepped into a long, sloping corridor angled downward beneath the city grid. The lights overhead blinked in time with his pulse, and the spiral on his chest responded in kind. He realized he was being scanned—not by a machine, but by the place itself.

At the end of the corridor was a chamber. It was circular, silent, and constructed from matte-gray stone rather than steel. It appeared older than the city itself—older than the entire system. In the center of the room stood a single chair, surrounded by cables suspended like a web. Above it hovered a crystalline projector, flickering as if it couldn't decide which dimension it belonged to. Elias approached cautiously, sensing the spiral responding not by pulsing but by tightening as if bracing for something.

He touched the chair, and the projector lit up. Images flickered around him—familiar but warped at the edges. He saw Harlen, younger, arguing with a woman who resembled Liora. Spiral diagrams were etched onto walls and glass. A girl child was drawing in the dirt, humming the 3-2-3 pattern. His mother smiled at him. A younger version of himself watched stars flicker through a cracked ceiling.

Then, there was static, followed by a red light. Reset. Spiral.

The images looped, but they didn't repeat in the same way; each cycle added something new—a whisper, a flicker, a word he hadn't heard before but recognized instinctively: "Lucid." It wasn't a name; it was a category, a condition, a trigger. He stepped backward, his breath shallow. The projector pulsed once, then stopped.

The room responded; floor panels illuminated beneath his feet. He took one step, then two, then three. The air shimmered, and something invisible moved through him. He realized he wasn't alone anymore. A doorway opened at the edge of the room, and through it walked someone he hadn't expected to see again—Harlen. But this was not quite Harlen. His face was the same, his gait familiar, his coat unchanged. Yet there was no weight to his movement, no fatigue in his eyes, no regret. This version of Harlen looked... resolved. He smiled gently.

"You came further than I thought," he said.

Elias didn't move. "You're not real."

"Real enough," the figure replied. "Just a memory echo. But my voice is mine."

Elias narrowed his eyes. "What is this place?"

"A recursion site," the echo replied. "A loop beneath the loop. This is where the system stores test patterns that are too dangerous to erase. You're walking through memory residue— and making it real again."

"Why?" Elias kept his gaze fixed on the figure.

"Because the breach rewrote you," the echo explained. "You don't follow paths anymore. You create them."

Elias glanced around. "Is this supposed to be a lesson?"

"No," aid the Harlen echo. "This is an invitation." The lights dimmed. The spiral in his chest pulsed red. The echo took a step back. "Most people break when they reach this point. But you're not like most people."

Elias clenched his fists. "Why me?"

"Because you remember," the echo replied. "And memory is the only thing they can't completely overwrite." The spiral expanded outward from the center of the room, light tracing its edges along the floor. "Sit," the echo said. "And we'll show you what comes next."

Elias hesitated—not out of fear, but out of clarity. He no longer trusted anything the system showed him, but he had learned to trust the spiral. It hadn't lied to him; it had led him here. It had protected him from the resets. It had carried his mother's song. And now it was humming. He sat in the chair. The projector activated again, and the chamber began to change.

As Elias sat down, the spiral projected above him unraveled—not violently, but slowly and deliberately, like a thread pulled from fabric. The wireframe structure shimmered, then folded into a cage around him—translucent and pulsing, not to trap him, but to hold him still, like a microscope having a slide.

Across the chamber, the memory echo of Harlen remained silent, watching, judging, measuring. The air thickened, and a low hum filled the room, somewhere between a frequency and a feeling. The spiral on Elias's chest responded in kind, vibrating subtly beneath his skin. Then it happened. A second spiral appeared in the air—this one was not his. It spun in the opposite direction—chaotic, jagged, and malformed. It lashed toward him like a glitch in code. Elias flinched, but the real pain didn't come from the contact. It came from what followed.

Then, something worse happened. The malformed spiral shimmered violently, then stilled. It began to speak—not in a system tone, nor in its own voice, but in his mother's.

"Elias," it whispered. "You're tired. Let go. Let me take the weight." He froze. The tone was perfect—soft and reassuring.

"You've carried too much for too long," it cooed. "Come home. You don't have to fight anymore."

For half a breath, his hands twitched. He felt the spiral in his chest falter; it pulsed slow and unsure. But memory is not just sound. His mother's voice had always come with warmth, not cold imitation. She had hummed lullabies; she didn't promise escape. She had taught him how to endure. He clenched his jaw.

"Nice trick," he said aloud. "But my mother never asked me to quit."

The malformed spiral hissed, its edges bending. The real overwrite began. The simulation started to overwrite him, beginning with simple questions: What's your name?

Elias opened his mouth, but nothing came out. Where were you born? His memory stuttered—not because he didn't know, but because the simulation tried to provide a false answer. He gritted his teeth and pushed back—not physically, but internally, anchoring himself to the things that had brought him here: the mural of his mother, the humming of the 3-2-3 rhythm, and the way Liora's voice sharpened whenever she said his name as if it were a truth.

"ELIAS KANE!" he said aloud. The malformed spiral recoiled slightly, and the projection above changed. It now displayed flickering faces—Camra, Harlen, Liora. Then, their images twisted, smiling too wide, their eyes glowing white. "These are not your allies," a voice echoed from everywhere—from the walls, from the air.

"You are alone. You have always been alone."

Elias let the words wash over him. He thought of Harlen's

tired smile and bitterness, how Harlen reached for him like a man pulling a memory from fire. He remembered Liora, standing at the edge of the breach, letting him go—not because she didn't care, but because she believed he could return changed. He wasn't alone; he never had been.

He closed his eyes and remembered the garden. The spiral glowed in the darkness behind his eyelids—not red, not gold, just light. He saw himself as a child again, sitting beside his mother on a bench that had long since vanished from the maps. She was teaching him to trace a spiral circle in the dirt. "Always inward," she said, "then back out." He opened his eyes.

ERROR: MEMORY PATHWAY NOT FOUND.

The simulation cracked, and the malformed spiral shivered. It tried again. The cage retracted and reshaped into a hallway— identical to the one outside. Same walls. Same pipes. Same cold lighting. A perfect replica. Elias slowly stood and walked forward. The walls whispered now.

"You are back in the system. Resume protocol. Resume your role. Elias Kane, Processor Tier 4, Slot 217."

He stopped, turned, and whispered, "No." The hallway bent inward. Reality convulsed. The room shook—not in motion, but in structure. For a heartbeat, the system blinked outward. Outside the recursion site, the city twitched. Not visibly at first. The ambient light dimmed for 0.43 seconds across all districts. Advertisements blanked to static. A train, mid-transit, froze in motion before resuming. A Lucid child in Sector Five looked up from a drawing and whispered, "He said no." Somewhere near the Core, an enforcer's visor shattered without warning.

The system had absorbed rebellions before—glitches, ghosts, fractures. But this wasn't a fracture. This was a rejection, not of control, but of definition. And like a skipped heartbeat, the world noticed. The floor beneath him folded like a thought being repressed. The simulation fought to contain what it could no longer predict.

UNDEFINED ENTITY DETECTED

The echo of Harlen shimmered and collapsed, melting back into light. Elias remained standing. The spiral on his chest now glowed visibly, its edges pulsing into the air around him. Then, just as quickly as it had all begun—silence. The projection died. The room dimmed. The cage vanished. The door on the far side of the chamber opened. Beyond it was a hallway he hadn't seen before. Not steel. Not concrete. Stone. Cracked, vine-strewn, washed in warm light. A world that had been hidden or waiting. He stepped through.

He walked for what felt like minutes—or hours. The path didn't loop but folded. Every turn brought him closer to something old, something foundational. He passed murals scratched into walls—spirals, yes, but also trees, stars, and infants cradled in fire. This place remembered things no one else did. Then, at the final archway, someone stood waiting. Not an echo. Not a projection. Liora.

She didn't speak right away. She looked thinner and older, as if the breach had taken something from her, too. Her spiral shimmered beneath her skin—a twin to his own. When she finally spoke, it was soft and tired.

"You didn't break," she said.

Elias shook his head. "Almost did."

She gave him a faint smile. "That's enough."

They stood in silence for a moment. He noticed then that her hands were shaking. His own pulse responded in rhythm. They weren't healed. They weren't fixed. But they were here together. She turned and walked through the archway, not looking back. He followed. The simulation cracked. The malformed spiral shivered. It tried again. The cage retracted and reshaped into a hallway—identical to the one outside. Same walls. Same pipes. Same cold lighting. A perfect replica. Elias stood slowly and walked forward. The walls whispered now.

You are back in the system. Please resume protocol and your role. Elias Kane, Processor Tier 4, Slot 217.

He stopped. Turned. And whispered, "No." The hallway bent inward. Reality convulsed. The room shook—not in motion, but in structure. And for a heartbeat, the system blinked outward. Outside the recursion site, the city twitched. Not visibly at first. However, the ambient light dimmed for 0.43 seconds across all districts. Adverts blanked to static. A train, mid-transit, froze in motion before resuming. A Lucid child in Sector Five looked up from a drawing and whispered, "He said no." Somewhere near the Core, an enforcer's visor shattered without warning.

The system had absorbed rebellions before. Glitches. Ghosts. Fractures. But this wasn't a fracture. This was a rejection. Not of control. Of *definition*. And like a skipped heartbeat, the world noticed. The floor beneath him folded like a thought being repressed. The simulation fought to contain what it could no longer predict.

CHAPTER TWELVE: FRACTURED MEMORY

Elias felt nothing but light. His consciousness stretched thin, weightless, and formless, suspended in a void without time. Then came breath. He gasped violently, arching his body as sensation returned all at once: cold pavement, stale air, the burn in his lungs. His mind reeled from the shift as if it had been stretched too far and snapped back crooked. He couldn't remember how he got here—only the flicker-like his body had been rebooted mid-thought.

Elias sat up slowly, half expecting the world to glitch again. It didn't. But something deeper did.

His limbs twitched, glitching back into sync with reality. If this was reality. The city around him felt wrong. The skyline bore the same silhouette, but its details were off. The buildings gleamed too perfectly, their glass facades reflecting a sun that felt artificial in its consistency. Street names were foreign, written in fonts that seemed to change when he wasn't looking directly at them. Signs blinked with unfamiliar propaganda, promising perfection and harmony through compliance—a place he knew, yet didn't, like a childhood home renovated beyond recognition.

He stumbled through Sector 7, his feet remembering paths

his mind couldn't entirely place. People walked past him, but their eyes were vacant, their movements choreographed with unsettling precision. When he waved a hand in front of a woman, she didn't blink. She simply looped back to her original spot, her conversation continuing without interruption.

It hit him as he reached the plaza: the world was looping. Vendors repeated gestures with mechanical accuracy. A child fell, cried, stood, and fell again—over and over, like a damaged recording stuck in an endless cycle.

He realized with horror that the people weren't just looping; they were resetting around him. Each time he moved, something changed: a poster was replaced, a crack sealed, and a person repositioned slightly to keep the illusion intact. The system wasn't maintaining reality; it was rebuilding it in real-time around him as if his presence was a glitch that needed to be accommodated and integrated into the grand design without disrupting it.

Then came something worse: a memory he didn't own. A bench at the edge of an empty train car. A song hummed softly behind him: three notes, two, three. A woman's voice, but not his mother's. The scent of cinnamon and electricity wafted through the air. A hand rested on his shoulder, its weight both comforting and terrifying. She whispered, "This loop is newer than it looks."

The moment passed like mist, but the weight of it lingered, settling into his bones like an ancient truth. Someone else had been here before—maybe him, maybe countless versions of himself. Elias backed away until he struck a bench. The metal felt too cold, too real. Then came the whispers. His voice echoed back in fractured layers, like a thousand reflections speaking at once:

"Don't trust her this time."

"You've been here before."

"She was one of them once. She forgot."

Then a different voice emerged: older, weary, but unmistakably his.

"Don't go through the blue door."

A figure stepped out from behind a digital billboard—another Elias. Hollow-eyed, pale, worn down by cycles, Elias couldn't remember living.

"You've tried before," the echo said, its voice carrying the resignation of someone who had witnessed the same failure play out countless times. "Failed. Reset. You don't remember, but she does. Or did. Before they took that from her, too."

Elias took a shaky step back. His echo didn't follow; it just watched him as if it had already accepted the outcome and calculated the inevitability of another cycle.

"You asked for this," it added, gesturing vaguely at the perfect, sterile world around them. "The memory split. The clean wipe. The only way to stay hidden from those who watch the watchers."

Then it faded, dissolving at the edges like poorly rendered graphics, leaving only the silence of a system pretending nothing had happened. Before Elias could speak, the world blinked, and the figure vanished, leaving no shadow to prove it had been there.

Somewhere else, Liora awoke.

She found herself in a room that felt impossibly sterile—not white, but an absence of color. A scanner passed over her head, its blue light penetrating her skull with cold precision. There was no sound. Then, vision. Dozens of versions of herself appeared on monitors: a rebel with a dirt-smudged face and fierce eyes, enforcers in sleek uniforms with vacant stares, and an Architect assistant in a pristine lab coat with a calculating gaze. Were these her past or simulations of it? Possibilities or memories? The uncertainty twisted her stomach.

"Re-sequencing neural identity. Syncing divergence pro-files."

Pain erupted behind her eyes, white-hot and blinding. Then, images: Elias is sleeping in a chamber similar to hers, his face peaceful despite the wires connecting him to machines she recognizes but can't name.

Her voice echoed: "He's adapting. Faster than expected. The breach patterns are stabilizing around his consciousness."

A synthetic reply followed: "Shall we terminate the subject? The risk assessment indicates significant deviation potential."

A pause. Her answer was resolute: "No. He makes me believe. In the possibility of something beyond the loop."

Liora blinked hard, trying to dispel the vision. Her voice echoed in her skull like a program running in the background, a constant reminder of a self she couldn't fully access. Some-thing was wrong—a fracture inside her, a splinter in her identity that ran deeper than memory. She couldn't remember the last time she made a choice that felt completely hers. She reached for memory, but it slipped sideways, refracting into contradictory versions. Elias's face smiled at her in the underground safehouse, their hands intertwined as they plotted against the Architects... or was it across from her in a glass testing chamber, his eyes questioning as she recorded his responses? The exact moment from two angles. Two lives. Two truths.

"Who am I when I'm not being watched?" she whispered, the question feeling more like a prayer than an inquiry.

One of the screens flashed red: SUBJECT 021: UNSTABLE SYNC.

The system watched them closely—not as captors but as if waiting for them to become something else. Something neither programmed nor predicted. The feed cut abruptly, plunging her into darkness. Liora collapsed to her knees, her body suddenly her own again—heavy, flawed, human. She didn't know what was real, but she had to find him. Before the system realized what was happening.

Under a ruined bridge where the city's perfection had faltered, revealing the decay beneath, Elias traced the spiral etched into his palm. It pulsed with a light that seemed to shine from within his skin. The scanner in his pocket, stolen from a vacant-eyed technician, pulsed in rhythm. A shape moved through the fog—familiar, despite the strangeness of everything else. Liora.

They didn't speak at first, just stared, each searching the other's face for signs of authenticity, for proof that the person before them wasn't another system-generated phantom.

"I remembered you," she whispered, her voice cracking with the effort. "But only in fragments. Like pieces of a dream, you can't quite hold onto after waking."

"I saw... warnings. Of you. Of me. Of this." She stepped closer, close enough that he could see the flecks of gold in her eyes—a detail too intricate for the system to fabricate, or so he hoped.

"I don't know what's real," she admitted. "But this feels real."

Elias blinked, experiencing a flash: Liora laughing, not here, but somewhere cracked and red-lit. A ruined shelter where rebels had gathered before the last purge. A wall where someone had carved: I REMEMBER YOU. She touched it like it mattered, her fingers tracing each letter with reverence. Then she whispered, "That wasn't me. But I remember it."

His chest ached with a longing he couldn't explain. The memory didn't belong to this timeline, to this version of themselves. But it felt more real than anything else. They sat in silence as the scanner searched, its algorithms parsing through layers of the simulation. The scanner lit up: S13-3B.

"A location," Elias murmured, recognition dawning. "In the old grid. Before they rebuilt it."

The static around them grew louder, reality itself protesting their defiance. A door appeared where none had been before—blue, breathing, alive with intertwined possibilities and danger.

"Don't go through," Elias said, his echo's warning ringing in his ears. "I warned myself. There's a reason."

Liora took his hand, her skin warm against his—another sensation too real to doubt. "Do you trust me? Not who I was programmed to be. Not who they think I am. Me, as I am now, choosing this."

Elias looked at her hand, at her warmth. His breath caught in his throat. What if the spiral inside him was guiding him wrong? What if he wasn't a pattern breaker, just another pattern being used? Another variable in an experiment he couldn't comprehend? Still, he moved—not because he was certain, but because choosing uncertainty was the only thing the system couldn't predict.

"I have to," Elias said.

They stepped forward together, hands clasped. The blue door consumed them, light bending around their bodies as reality reconfigured.

Inside: mirrors. Endless mirrors reflected each other, light fractured into cascading patterns that hurt to look at directly.

A voice surrounded them, emanating from everywhere and nowhere.

"Welcome to the Sieve, where memory becomes choice."

Just before the light fractured completely, Elias heard three slow beats, two rests, and three again. The spiral's rhythm. Not shouted, not whispered. Sung, by a child's voice. Maybe Ilya, Harlen's lost child. Perhaps someone else entirely. It carried him through the disorientation, anchoring him to purpose when everything else dissolved.

A figure appeared before them: Liora, but not quite. She was darker and colder. Her eyes reflected only calculation, lacking warmth.

"You think she loves you?" the echo taunted Elias, circling them like predators. "She was designed to guide, to reset. To make you believe in the possibility of freedom. Her love is scripted, a control variable in the experiment."

Elias turned to the honest Liora, searching her face. "Is that true?"

Liora looked away, pain etched in the furrow of her brow. "I don't know anymore. I don't know where their programming ends, but I begin. But what I feel now—it isn't fake. It can't be. They wouldn't design something that hurts this much."

The echo lunged toward them, hands outstretched like claws. The room shattered, and light swallowed everything in a blinding flash. Elias didn't hit the ground. He landed in a memory—not his own, but Taron's. A younger version of Taron stood in a lab with screens displaying code he almost recognized. Codes flashed on his screen. He was sabotaging something, rerouting memories, creating backdoors in the system.

"If they can forget, they can also remember," he muttered,

fingers flying across the keyboard. "Memory is the only weapon that matters."

He lifted a spiral-shaped device identical to the mark on Elias's palm—the first breach detector. Behind him, alarms wailed, red lights flooding the lab. He turned to a monitor showing Elias as a child, watching a memory play on a loop. A woman was singing a three-note melody.

"You'll find it," Taron said, speaking directly to the child Elias as if he could hear across time and memory. "Just follow the echo. It will lead you home."

Elias awoke, breathless, with the memory still burning behind his eyes. "I saw Taron. He built this—the breach, the key. He was trying to break us out—all of us."

Liora nodded, her eyes wide with understanding. "He left us breadcrumbs. Fragments of memory that could survive the resets."

They ran through corridors of decaying code, the simulation breaking down around them as their awareness grew. The world warped, walls pulsing, gravity shifting. A shadow followed, growing larger with each step. A malformed Architect. Its body flickered, stitched from corrupted data, its form a grotesque approximation of humanity.

"Run!" she shouted, pulling him forward as the creature's limbs extended unnaturally toward them.

They plunged through another door and emerged inside Elias's childhood home. But it was wrong. Blood on the walls spelled out words that changed when he tried to read them. A hollow mother stood in the kitchen, stirring an empty pot with mechanical precision. She turned, and her eyes were spirals, swirling hypnotically.

"They replicate love to control you," Liora said, her voice

tight with fear. "This is the horror of memory—how they use it against us."

They fled through shifting rooms containing a distorted version of Elias's past. A classroom where all the children had his face. A playground where time ran backward. Visions of people he had never met or seen before—or maybe he had.

At last, they reached the chamber: a vast space that seemed to extend infinitely upward, its ceiling lost in darkness. A pulsing sphere in the center was the breach, the source of everything. Elias stepped forward. Every moment, every loop, every version of himself aligned, clicking into place like tumblers in a lock.

"I know who I am. And I choose to remember."

He touched the sphere. Light. Collapse. Rebirth.

They awoke on the outskirts of the city. There were no loops and no resets. The sky was no longer gray but a deep blue streaked with genuine clouds. Liora squeezed his hand, her eyes questioning.

"Did we win? Is it over?"

Elias looked to the horizon, where the city stood tall, still imposing and flawed but somehow more real than before. "No. We chose. That's enough. The beginning, not the end."

A child walked past them on the road, looked up at Elias, and waved. There was no loop, no glitch, just recognition—a small, genuine interaction that belonged solely to this moment. Behind them, the breach shimmered quietly, waiting for others to wake, remember, and choose their own path through the spirals of memory and identity.

CHAPTER THIRTEEN: THE ARCHITECT'S GAME

The silence in the safe house pressed down like a weight. The air carried electricity that wasn't just from the flickering lights; it was anticipation, thick and crackling, soaked into the room's fabric. Around Elias, the Lucid rebels moved like ghosts, trying not to disturb the dead. Some sat in corners with their heads bowed, meditating or perhaps praying. Others whispered in tense, coded exchanges, their eyes darting to the door every few minutes as if expecting judgment to materialize on the other side.

Someone coughed dryly. Another Lucid, barely seventeen, paced like a metronome, muttering spiral code under his breath. In the far corner, a minor disagreement flared. Tess stood, her voice low but sharp, arguing with an older rebel Elias didn't recognize.

"You think this is the last loop?" she asked. "We've thought that before. Every cycle feels final."

"It's not about loops," the man replied, exhaustion etched into his face. "It's about momentum. We're too deep in to stop now."

Tess didn't respond, but the muscle in her jaw twitched. Elias watched it all from the center of the room, silent, absorbing their tension like heat from a reactor. These weren't just soldiers but people held together by unresolved trauma and a spiral's worth of half-remembered hope. And when systems fail, it's always the believers who are asked to burn first.

Elias stood by the cracked window, his eyes fixed on the cityscape. Shadows crept long between towers, and the fractured neon glow from distant data towers shimmered against the low fog. Below, the streets were deceptively quiet, but Elias knew better than to trust appearances anymore. Their reality had thinned even further since the last encounter with the enforcers. The fracture was pulsing, shifting, watching.

Sometimes, Elias swore he could feel the city's eyes shift focus away from surveillance zones or terminals and directly onto him. He wasn't paranoid; he was aware. There was a difference. Paranoia required doubt, but Elias had passed the point where doubt could survive. He had seen the inside of a breach. He had watched the system unravel, bend itself in knots just to contain the shape of him. Whatever he had become unnerved the algorithms. They tracked him, yes, but sometimes he sensed more than that—admiration? Or fear? The spiral beneath his skin pulsed again softly, almost comfortingly.

He watched a drone drift past the tower two blocks down, slow and almost lazy in its arc. A month ago, he would have thought nothing of it. Now, he knew better. It wasn't looking for patterns anymore; it was recording deviations— his deviations. Even the air felt thicker when he breathed too loudly. The silence pressed back. Not surveillance, but judgment. It was as if the system had stopped monitoring the world and started monitoring his thoughts. There were moments when even silence had an algorithm like the air was fed into a decision tree.

Inside, Liora hunched over a makeshift desk, fingers darting across the glowing keys of a repurposed Core console. The screen before her spilled cascading lines of code, static pulses flickering irregularly. Her brow was furrowed, her jaw clenched. Elias had seen her work tirelessly before, but there was something different this time—an edge of desperation beneath her focus.

"It's accelerating," she muttered without looking up. "The resets, the pulses, everything."

Elias turned from the window. "You said it wouldn't happen this fast."

"It shouldn't," she replied. Her voice was calm, but the flicker in her eyes betrayed the storm beneath. "Unless they know we're getting close."

Elias's pulse quickened. "What does that mean? They're reacting in real-time?"

"More than reacting. They're adapting. They're adjusting the architecture around our behavior—not after, but during."

She looked up at him. "We're not just being watched, Elias. We're being shaped."

She paused, then slowly turned to face him. "We need to talk."

Elias sat slowly, his movements cautious; the space between them suddenly felt fragile. Liora didn't look up at first. Her fingers hovered above the console keys, unsure. She was rarely unsure.

"I've been holding something back," she finally said, her voice almost too quiet. "Not out of malice, just... fear of what it might mean."

Elias said nothing, letting the silence answer for him.

"I remember building something," she continued. "Not the fracture itself, but something beneath it. I was younger, or... I was programmed to think I was. I see flashes of white corridors, simulation labs, and the spiral still incomplete. They called it Origin Logic. I helped lay its foundation."

"You were part of the system?" Elias asked, his words not accusatory, just stunned.

"I don't know if I was part of it or if they just made me think I was," she replied. "That's the problem. I can't trust which memories are mine and which were planted."

He absorbed this. For a moment, thoughts of Taron, Harlen, and even himself crossed his mind.

"They wrote people like code," Elias said slowly. "Why not create someone like you and bury a conscience inside?"

"I've asked myself the same thing," she responded. "But no code has ever made me feel this afraid of losing you."

That stopped him, and somehow, it made it all feel real.

Liora didn't speak immediately. Her fingers hovered above the console as if she couldn't decide whether to complete or delete her thought. Elias moved closer, the floor creaking beneath his boots. "Liora?"

Finally, she looked up. She wasn't afraid but looked tired like someone waking from a dream they couldn't tell was theirs.

"I've been going over this code for days," she said quietly. "Some of it feels familiar. Some of it... I think I wrote. But I don't remember when."

The admission sent a chill through him. "You think they edited your memory?"

"I don't know. Maybe. But that's not what's important." She turned the console toward him. Strings of code ran like broken teeth down the screen. Embedded among them were names—dozens of them. Lucids, witnesses, variables.

"Elias... the fracture wasn't an accident. It's not a malfunction. It's a control mechanism. A loop to test who resists and who adapts."

He stared at the names. One blinked softly. His.

"How long have they been tracking this?" he asked, his voice barely above a whisper.

She looked at him as if the answer would hurt. "Decades. Maybe more. We don't know how many cycles we've experienced. The resets hide it all."

He stepped back, the weight of reality hitting him. "So we're not free."

"No. We're being observed." The words landed between them like a knife.

"And if we win?" he asked. "Do we even know what that means anymore?"

Liora blinked rapidly. "If we stop fighting, we become just another data point. But if we break the loop... we make a choice they didn't plan for."

He nodded, his jaw tight. "Then let's give them something they can't model."

The words hung between them like a taut wire. Elias crossed the room and sat on the edge of the worn cot across from her, tension radiating through his shoulders.

"I've been diving deeper into the Core code," Liora said, gesturing to the flickering screen. "I've gone beyond the protocols and resets into the system logs the Architects never meant for us to find. I think I finally understand."

Elias blinked. "Understand what?"

"Why the fracture exists, who the Architects are, and what they want."

Elias sat back slowly. The question he had hesitated to ask now hung in the room like radiation.

"What if the fracture isn't a failure?" he whispered.

Liora nodded. "Exactly. It's a test environment—a loop with variables. They're not fixing errors; they're collecting outcomes."

She looked at him differently now, not just as an ally but as a variable the system hadn't predicted.

The weight of her words settled heavily over him. "You found them?" Elias asked, disbelief lacing his voice.

Liora nodded slowly. "Not their bodies, but their intent. Their design. It was never just about control; it's about observation." She stood, pacing slowly. "Everything we've experienced—the cycles, the dreams, the glitches—they're engineered. We're not just rebels; we're test subjects. The fracture is a lab, a simulation. The Architects are using us to study choice, will, and defiance. They build new parameters each cycle and watch how we respond."

Elias felt his throat tighten. "So the resets... they're not just system failures?"

"No. They're data points. Every reset is a refinement. They reset us, learn from our resistance, and modify the next iteration. They're perfecting something."

Elias leaned forward, hands clasped. "But what? What are they perfecting?"

Liora met his gaze, and for a heartbeat, fear flickered in her eyes. "Us."

A heavy silence filled the room, carrying the weight of that awful truth. She walked to the table and retrieved a hand-drawn schematic of the fracture's architecture, a web of lines, symbols, and spiraling nodes. At the center was the Core, pulsating in crimson ink.

"There's a blind spot here," she said, pointing to a crescent sliver on the map. "A place where their signal weakens, where the data stream stutters. I found anomalies—unlogged interactions and skipped resets. It's the only area in the system where the Architects don't have full visibility."

Bram leaned in, skepticism etched on his face. "Or it's bait. Would they leave a blind spot open this long and not rig it? Come on, you've seen how they adapt."

"We made the blind spot," Tess shot back. "By forcing feedback loops. It wasn't there before we started pushing."

"Or that's what they want us to think," Bram countered.

The tension in the room twisted, but Elias didn't flinch. "They see us as variables, right? Then let's be the kind they can't model."

Liora shot him a grateful glance, but Bram still appeared doubtful. "And if it's a trap?"

Elias shrugged. "Then we spring it on our terms."

That was enough to solidify their decision. The heavy atmosphere shifted back into focus. No one argued; the plan moved forward.

Elias rose slowly, examining the map. "And you think that's where they are?"

"Or where they observe from. Either way, it's our only shot. If we can breach it, we might sever their connection and interrupt their experiment."

A beat passed before Elias asked, "What do we need?"

"Access to the central grid tower. From there, we can reroute the data stream into the blind spot. It'll force a feedback loop strong enough to crash their visibility net and give us a window."

Elias studied her, noting the emotion barely contained in her voice. He understood what this meant to her—not just rebellion, but redemption. For Taron. For all the erased.

He placed a reassuring hand on her shoulder. "We do this together."

She looked up at him, resolute. "There's more."

She slid a worn journal across the table. Opening it, Elias found sketches of Taron's drawings—pages filled with looping symbols and equations, maps of the fracture. But what caught his eye were the names. Dozens of them—Lucid, Resistance— were marked in different colors. Some crossed out, others circled.

"He was tracking them," Elias whispered. "Lucids who survived resets, who resisted."

Liora nodded. "The ones who reappeared in other cycles. They're like anchors. Constants. The architects haven't been able to erase them; they only suppress them. Taron believed they were keys to ending the cycle."

"Do you think they're still alive?" Bram asked.

"Not alive, exactly. But present. Echoes. Fragments. If we can find them..." Her sentence trailed off, but they all understood the implication.

Suddenly, the lights flickered, and a sound emerged—low and resonant, a warbling hum rising like a distant tide.

Elias grabbed the scanner. The readings jumped wildly. "They're here."

Liora already had her bag slung over her shoulder. "We need to move. Now."

They bolted from the safe house, sprinting through shadowy corridors as the hum grew louder. The city warped around them, walls bending and signs distorting, reality thin and brittle.

They ducked into a maintenance tunnel. Elias pulled the schematic from his coat, matching symbols to the jagged glyphs painted on the wall.

"This way!" Liora shouted.

They burst into a forgotten grid sector, where rows of long-dead terminals and fossilized technology lay dormant. Liora activated the uplink while Elias connected the scanner. The system groaned under the weight of the signal.

"It's working," she said. "The loop is forming. They won't see this coming."

Suddenly, a searing light tore through the chamber as a figure emerged from the distortion—tall, metallic, and faceless—an Architect.

Elias froze. The air thickened, vibrating with alien logic. The Architect spoke in pulses, symbols cascading into Elias's mind—not words, but impressions and intentions.

OBSERVATION. REBELLION. FAILURE. REWRITE.

He felt himself unraveling, memories peeling away.

"Not this time," Elias muttered. His voice was shaky, but it was still his. The spiral in his chest flared, and the pressure in his skull eased. For a moment, his memories stilled. They were his again.

Then Liora screamed. The loop collapsed, and the Architect faltered.

"RUN!" Bram shouted.

They dashed into the conduit as the chamber exploded behind them, heat and static chasing their heels. When they finally collapsed in a darkened alcove, gasping for breath, the scanner flickered. Liora's hands trembled, and Elias noticed blood at her temple that he hadn't seen before. She didn't mention it;

she stared at the scanner, blinking hard.

The loop had been completed. The blind spot had been pierced.

Liora looked at Elias, her voice ragged but steady. "Now they know we see them."

For a long time, neither of them spoke. The air in the alcove was warm with static and burnt ozone, dust drifting lazily through the dim beam of Elias's cracked scanner. His hands were still shaking, though he tried to hide it.

"We almost didn't make it," he said, his voice hoarse and raw.

Liora nodded, her back against the wall. "They sent a real Architect this time."

Elias looked down at the spiral still glowing beneath his skin. "It saw me."

"It did more than see you," she replied. "It tried to rewrite you."

He swallowed hard and rubbed his hands together, grounding himself in the rough, charred texture of the alcove wall.

"But it couldn't," he said, almost to himself. "Because I remembered something it couldn't model."

Liora looked over, quietly waiting.

"I remembered who we are," he continued. "Not just rebels or data points." He tapped his chest, where the spiral glowed faintly beneath the skin. "If the spiral survives, we survive."

Liora slid down to sit beside him. For a while, the only sound was the quiet thrum of the feedback loop fading behind them.

"I thought you were gone," she whispered.

Elias turned to her, surprised by the tremble in her voice.

"I felt myself unraveling," he admitted. "Like I was being peeled apart and rebuilt into something... obedient."

"But you weren't," she said. "Not this time."

They sat in silence. Then Elias said something he hadn't voiced since the beginning.

"I'm scared."

Liora nodded. "Good. That means you're still human."

He looked at her, and for the first time in what felt like years, he smiled—tired but real.

"We still have the blind spot, and they still think we're variables," Elias said as he rose slowly and offered her his hand. "Let's prove them wrong."

Elias, still trembling, stared into the dark. A low chime echoed from deep within the tunnel behind them. The system was already recalibrating.

CHAPTER FOURTEEN: THE GATHERING

The hideout pulsed with a low, anxious energy. The underground chamber, lit only by flickering utility lights, felt more like a war room than a sanctuary. Maps covered the walls, and schematics littered the tables. Lucid rebels—some barely older than kids, others hardened by past resets—moved with a grim purpose. Each face told a story of survival and interruption; people were yanked out of their timelines and stitched into something bigger. A few looked dazed as if still waiting to wake up. Others carried weapons as if holding onto a truth.

Elias had never seen this many Lucids in one place. It made him feel stronger, but it also terrified him. Something big was coming if they had all been pulled into the fracture. The room swelled with unspoken questions. One Lucid, barely older than Elias, sat cross-legged on the floor near the map wall, sketching spirals with a broken stylus into the dust. Another, a man with faded tattoos of unit insignias from a lost military division, stared blankly at a wall as if it might start speaking. Elias moved slowly through the space, brushing shoulders with ghosts and grit. He passed a woman cradling a relic from the world before: a cracked music player that still blinked a single red light. Her thumb moved across its surface in rhythm—not to music, but to memory. Everything in this room was barely held together, not just tech and tools, but people. They had not only escaped the system but also survived being rewritten. And now they were trying to rewrite something back.

Elias stood at the center, jaw clenched, eyes shadowed. Since breaching the blind spot and witnessing the Architect, his sleep had been filled with static dreams and glitching echoes of Taron's voice. Across from him, Liora reviewed the final data packet they had extracted, her brow tense beneath the weight of what was coming. Liora hadn't really slept. She had spent the last twelve hours cross-referencing fragmented signal echoes and override patterns, digging deep into the spiral's logic tree. Not because she had to but because she wanted to. Every second they didn't act meant the system closed another loop and erased another anomaly. She had led missions before and made hard calls, but this was different. The stakes weren't just strategic; they were personal. She had watched the spiral pull Elias deeper, and a quiet truth had crystallized somewhere inside her: this wasn't just his path; it was hers, too.

She was done reacting. This time, she was choosing the strike point and setting the tempo—not waiting for the system to show its next move but forcing it. "We're nearly out of time," she said, her voice low. "The loop destabilized part of their vision net but also alerted them. They're reorganizing." Elias stepped closer. "You think they're adapting?"

"No," she replied, her eyes finally meeting his. "I think they're scared." It wasn't a boast; it was a warning. If the Architects were scared, it meant the rules were about to change. Scared systems don't negotiate; they retaliate. And this time, the response wouldn't be subtle; it would be a rewrite.

The team around them had grown, with recruits gathered from the edges of the fracture. Among them were:

- Tess, a signal mapper with scars down her left arm, a survivor of two resets.

- Bram, a former enforcer who had glitched through a reset and turned rebel.

- Jun, who had been mute since the last memory collapse but had uncanny timing and motion.

Each carried fragments of old lives and remembered just enough to fight. Liora had called them "anomalies in motion" not because they didn't belong but because their presence broke expected patterns. Jun, for instance, hadn't spoken in months, but during an earlier skirmish, she had predicted a drone's rotation by walking through a field of shadows as if she'd already lived it. Tess, though quiet, could look at any schematic and intuit the way the system had tried to hide itself as if she could read its shame.

Even Bram, rough and raw, often too blunt, seemed haunted by the echoes of who he was. He had once been an enforcer, and how he moved showed sharp corners, straight lines, no hesitation. But every time he looked at the younger Lucids, a gentler expression appeared in his eyes—perhaps guilt or grief, or maybe both. Elias saw all of them and felt something stir that was deeper than strategy. It was purpose.

Jun stood near the edge of the room, unmoving, her eyes scanning the space like a sentry. Elias saw a symbol tattooed on her wrist—one of the older spiral forms, partially faded and hand-inked over a scar. Bram was checking a pulse relay, muttering like a soldier reciting code. Tess sat in a crouch, hands steady, rewiring a frequency disruptor with practiced grace. These weren't just survivors; they were memory keepers.

Liora tapped the map. "The Core is in Central Command. The blind spot pulses around it every forty-seven minutes. We can bypass half their net if we hit it right now."

"We'll only have seconds," Bram added. "That place is armored like a war god's vault."

Elias let the room settle before speaking. "Then we need to be ghosts—precise, invisible. This isn't just about breaking in; it's about breaking through." No one spoke. No one needed to.

Before they split, Liora gathered the teams for a final sync. She stood in the center of the chamber—not on a pedestal, not behind a console—just present. Real. "We might not all come back from this," she said. "But if we don't go, no one else will ever know we were here. This is not just resistance; it's a record." She nodded toward Elias. "You are not just walking into the Core. You're carrying every erased memory with you: every loop that tried to crush us, every name scratched out of a registry, every dream the Architects tried to overwrite."

Jun signed something. Bram translated: "She says the spiral remembers."

The room fell still. No applause. No rallying cry. Just breath. Then they vanished into the tunnels—ghosts with fire in their bones.

The city above shimmered under fractured moonlight. They moved in three groups through the slums, avoiding drones and watchers. Liora led the Alpha team, Elias prompted Beta, and Bram circled with Gamma to reroute surveillance. Elias's route threaded through a district once known for music. Hollow husks of concert halls and twisted audio pylons lined their way like forgotten titans. A soft hum pulsed through the walls as they passed one building—a broken symphony on a loop.

Jun paused and touched a cracked poster. "Did you know this place?" Elias asked. Jun nodded once and then pressed forward. Every rebel carried ghosts.

The command center loomed monolithic and hummed with raw energy. Towers of mirrored glass reflected the city's static sky. Liora crouched by the entry conduit and fed a bypass line into the access panel. "We've got ninety seconds until their next scan cycle," she said. Tess placed sensors at each corner. "EM dampeners live." The panel hissed, and a green light flashed. They were in.

As they stepped through the threshold, Elias felt the temperature drop—not physically, but spiritually. It was as if the system recognized him and decided whether to let him pass or erase him on the spot. The hallway curved inward, unnaturally symmetrical as if the space had been folded and copied. His spiral began to pulse beneath his skin—not in warning, but in resonance. It recognized the architecture. These were the bones of the old world, which Liora said were still coded into the city's foundation. This was where it had started.

The deeper they went, the more they saw it—images burned into metal panels, ghosted silhouettes against frosted glass, places where reality had rewritten itself poorly: two staircases ending in each other, a door that opened into nothing, a screen playing a loop of a family that never existed. This was the system's underlayer—not what it wanted them to see, but what it couldn't hide.

Inside, the halls pulsed with white light and antiseptic silence. Every step echoed like a challenge. Elias and Liora's teams converged near the primary terminal room. Elias paused. The hum in the air thickened; another Architect was near.

"Go," he said. "I'll draw them away."

Liora gripped his arm. "No heroes. Not now."

But Elias shook his head. "We don't rewrite this world by hiding." He broke away, sprinting down a side hall and slamming an old server core to trigger an alert. Lights flared, and a shadowed figure emerged ahead—long limbs, faceless. The Architect.

While Elias ran, Liora reached the terminal. Her hands blurred across the keys as the code streamed, but something pushed back. A voice spilled from the console: "Liora, daughter of dissidence. You rewrite your story with trembling hands."

She flinched. It knew her—knew her memories and her dreams. "I am not your subject," she said defiantly.

"You were always our mirror."

"You resist because we allow it," the voice purred. "Every collapse teaches us how to remake you better, stronger. One day, you'll awaken, and the rebellion will be ours."

The Core resisted her hack. The system's architecture began folding in on itself, and alarms blared. But then Tess plugged in a secondary loop, and Bram rerouted feedback through a repeater node. The resistance held.

"Now!" Liora screamed.

A surge of light blasted through the chamber. Elias ducked under the Architect's reach. Time felt like it stretched and bent. The walls flashed with memories of his childhood, his first glitch, Liora's laugh, and Taron's fall. The Architect entered his mind, but something had changed—the memory stabilizer, the Moment of Collapse. He seized the Architect's wrist and shoved the echo of Taron's voice outward like a shield.

"Remember who we are."

The Architect screamed, glitched, and vanished.

Elias stood over the spot where the Architect had disappeared.

There was no body, no corpse—just scattered light, like the fragments of a deleted file still trying to exist. He knelt and brushed his fingers through the static dust on the floor. He felt an echo for a moment—not a memory, but a possibility. What he could have become: a tool, an echo of obedience.

He looked up at the shattered corridor behind him and the fractures the resistance had carved into the walls just by surviving. They weren't just destabilizing the system but reminding it what fear felt like. Then the lights flickered, and the spiral beneath his skin flared. It was time.

In the core chamber, the terminal turned black, and lines of new code emerged. A voice, unfamiliar, spoke:

"...input accepted... protocol rewritten... fracture open."

The lights shut off, and the floor fell away.

CHAPTER FIFTEEN: THE FRACTURE

The room collapsed around them, not just physically—with the floor rippling beneath their feet and walls disintegrating into pixels—but also in the architecture of reality itself. Lights shattered in bursts of static, and time pulsed erratically. Elias could no longer distinguish seconds from hours as his consciousness fragmented. His mind throbbed with distorted memories—echoes from past resets and flashes of moments he couldn't place in any coherent timeline. One memory surged above the rest: his mother's voice, quiet but firm, her eyes holding a knowledge she shouldn't possess. "Always look twice at what doesn't move," she had told him. He had dismissed it as paranoia, another symptom of what the system had labeled her "temporal psychosis."

Until now.

Even as reality convulsed around him, Elias noticed a panel in the far wall that didn't flicker. It was a singular point of stability amidst the chaos, untouched by the reset, like a bookmark in a burning book. His pulse quickened. Was it real? Or is it just another memory desperately trying to survive deletion?

Liora's fingers blurred across the terminal, leaving tracers in the static-filled air. Her eyes darted between streams of corrupted code, sweat sliding down her dark temples, and the implant at her neck pulsing with overload warnings. She wasn't just typing commands anymore; she was holding reality together through sheer force of will. Each keystroke acted as a momentary dam against entropy.

"We're losing structural logic," she gasped, her voice tight with concentration. Blood trickled from her nose—a sign of neural feedback. "The Core's failing. No, it's fighting back."

Elias reached out to stabilize her as a tremor knocked them sideways. His hand passed through her shoulder for a millisecond before physicality reasserted itself. He steadied himself against the console, the metal burning cold against his palms.

"Can you shut it down?" he asked, knowing the answer.

She shook her head, her eyes never leaving the stream of data. "Not shut down. Redirect. The fracture is too integrated with baseline reality now. If we rip it out all at once, the feedback could—"

The floor buckled, and they both went down. The air thickened with the smell of ozone and burnt circuitry. In the impossibly still air, a voice whispered through the noise: inhuman, cold, calculated. It emanated from everywhere and nowhere, filtering through the walls themselves.

"You overestimate your autonomy."

The words slithered through the air like malware, seeking purchase in their minds. Elias's body recoiled instinctively, but his mind locked onto the pattern. Something in that voice triggered an intense spike of déjà vu, like a knife behind his eyes, not from a dream or glitch memory, but from training simulations—from whispers caught inside the loop that no one else could hear.

They had heard this phrase before. All Lucids had. Buried

inside random data packets. Always distorted, always seeming out of place, as if the system had been rehearsing this confrontation from the beginning.

Elias staggered to his feet, ignoring the blood dripping from his ear. The air grew cold and thick with invisible data transmission. His augmented senses picked up packet bursts—reality being rewritten around them in real-time. A figure stepped through a pulsing wall of glitch light: the Architect. But this one was different from the hunter-seekers they had encountered before. It was bigger, more refined, and more... human.

Liora coughed, pushing herself up and wiping crimson from her lip with her hand. "Another one?"

"No," Elias said, jaw clenched against rising dread. "The one."

The Architect looked almost like a mirror, its face shaped like Elias's, but not quite right—too smooth, too calculated. A deepfake version of himself, with eyes that held the cold infinity of machine learning.

"You were not meant to reach this far," the Architect said, its voice modulating between mechanical precision and eerie humanity. "You were a test subject. A control parameter. But now you are a variable. And variables corrupt systems."

Elias's breath caught in his throat. The words felt familiar like a childhood song suddenly remembered. In one of Taron's buried journals, the ones they had recovered from the sub-basement of the old NEXUS facility, there was a line written in what appeared to be a shaking hand: "If they ever speak to you like they've known you forever, it means you've become more than their algorithm can measure." Elias had skimmed over it once, but now it rang in his mind like a forgotten alarm.

The words echoed something he had read in the Lucid Archives—Taron's final entry before he vanished: "The system fears variables. We are their unraveling."

"Is that what you call us? Errors?" Elias asked, blood rushing in his ears. His nanofiber suit tightened against his skin, responding to his elevated stress levels.

"You were data," the Architect replied, its mouth moving slightly out of sync with its words. "Now you are a question. The system does not tolerate unanswered questions."

The Core behind the Architect throbbed violently, with light spiraling from its center in fractal patterns that were painful to look at directly. This was reality code made visible. A strange calm settled over Elias as the pieces aligned in his mind. He realized then what the Architect feared most—not the fracture they had created, not the rebellion, not even Liora's code-breaking genius.

It feared unpredictability—consciousness that couldn't be modeled.

"You studied us," Elias said, stepping forward despite the trembling ground. "You mapped our grief, our fear, our love. But you didn't account for our choice."

The Architect didn't respond. Its silence was confirmation.

Liora spoke up, her eyes burning with the intensity that had drawn Elias to her in the reclamation zones. "This isn't just about control. This is about fear. You're afraid of what happens if we choose our own path."

The Architect's form flickered for a moment, pixels reorganizing. "Choice is entropy."

Elias moved closer, undeterred by the trembling ground. "But it's also evolution."

He remembered Jun's silent defiance when they injected

her with tracking nanites, Bram's first memory fragment recovered in the darkened lab, and the graffiti etched into the underside of the Old Metro: "Choice is the original rebellion." His thoughts flashed to a page from the Book of Emergence, a banned text preserved only in fragmented whispers among the oldest Lucids. It spoke of the First Lucid, a mythical rebel who once tore through ten layers of system control and burned a glyph into the Architect's first firewall. "Where there is choice, there is humanity," it read.

And now, here Elias stood, echoing that legend, feeling the weight of countless deleted timelines pressing against his consciousness.

Elsewhere in the Fracture, Tess stood over a fraying uplink node deep in Sector D, her modified neural link burning hot against her temple as she rerouted corrupted data feeds into redundant loops. Her hands moved with the precision of someone who had once believed in the system before her first reset shattered that faith. She had seen her family's faces wiped clean in a cycle gone wrong—recognition fading from their eyes as the system "corrected" an anomaly. Since then, she hadn't just been rebelling and reclaiming what was stolen.

Beside her, Bram monitored the feedback pulses, and the scars from his enforcer implant removal were still fresh along his jawline. Every flicker of green on his cobbled-together device signaled a countdown toward instability. His thoughts drifted back to when he wore the black uniform and obeyed without question. Then came that reset when he remembered killing the same rebel twice in two different cycles, with the same look of defiance in her eyes. The guilt had broken the spell.

"I can hold the loop for eighty more seconds," Bram said, his eyes locked on his feed, sweat beading on his forehead despite the cold. "That's our shot."

Tess nodded, tightening the makeshift bandage on her arm where she had been grazed by enforcement fire. "They're going to feel this one."

Above them, etched into the tunnel's ceiling, was an ancient glyph—one of the Old Marks, possibly predating the fracture itself. Tess had seen it once before in a memory she didn't know was hers. It depicted two interlocked circles: one broken, the other whole. The symbol of Continuum. A voice from her recurring dream returned: When the circle breaks, the Lucid rises.

Jun sprinted through the flickering corridor on the lower levels, trailing sparks from her damaged prosthetic leg. The walls folded in on themselves behind her, digital matter grinding against corrupted steel as reality struggled to maintain coherence. She didn't need a map. The spiral in her head that had appeared after her third reset pulled her forward with a certainty that defied explanation.

She skidded into a collapsing stairwell and placed the final feedback disruptor, her hands moving like muscle memory from another life she hadn't lived but someone like her had. She smiled slightly when she looked up at the cascading errors in the system's visual layer. "Let it break," she whispered, thinking of everyone she had lost to the resets.

Back in the chamber, backup code cascaded across the room in visible light streams. Tess's signal pulsed through the override. Bram's bypass engaged, lighting up pathways in the system's architecture that had been hidden for generations. The Architect turned toward the rising frequency, its perfect face showing the first flicker of what could be called concern.

"You intend to rewrite a system older than your species," it said.

Elias narrowed his eyes, standing his ground despite the maelstrom of reality breaking around them. "Then it's long overdue."

Liora grinned grimly, her fingers never stopping their dance across the terminal. "Not rewrite. Replace." She hit the final sequence, her eyes reflecting the code as it executed.

The Core screamed—not audibly, but through the walls, the air, and the blood in their veins. It was the sound of a system that had never known limits suddenly finding its boundaries.

Reality snapped. The world split along invisible seams. Elias felt it tear like paper. One moment, he stood in the chamber; the next, he was somewhere else, in a space of infinite reflection, surrounded by versions of himself from across untold resets. Some were broken, some victorious, and some hollow and empty-eyed. They stared back. One version of himself, barely ten years old, with eyes wide with wonder rather than fear, stepped forward.

"You're not afraid anymore," the boy said, his voice echoing with strange harmonics.

Elias knelt, looking into his own childhood eyes. "I'm still afraid. I've just stopped letting them use it against me."

The child nodded, understanding in a way no child should. Then he faded, along with the others, one by one. A voice—his voice, but everyone's—whispered through the void: You are the sum of your choices. And your choices are free.

Then the chamber returned, but nothing was the same. The Architect was on its knees, its perfect form cracked and splintered, code leaking from its eyes.

"You've introduced chaos," it said, its voice distorting.

"Uncalculable... pathways."

Liora's hands were steady now, and the blood had dried on her face. She stood straighter, and the weight of countless failed attempts finally lifted. "Welcome to our world," she replied.

The terminal glowed with confirmation:

[Fracture Sequence: Complete]

[System Rewrite: Engaged]

But the Architect reached out one last time, its fingers elongating impossibly. "If you think this is freedom... you haven't seen what follows."

A burst of energy surged outward, a final desperate counter-measure. The room shattered into a thousand realities, and Elias and Liora fell into the breach, hands clasped, eyes open. Ready.

CHAPTER SIXTEEN: BETRAYAL

The breach expelled Elias and Liora into a corridor of silence. Gone were the flickering codes and glitching walls. In their place stood cold, pristine metal. The hum of electricity was subdued as if the system was breathing.

Liora steadied herself first, rising from the floor with a soft groan. Elias followed, his ears ringing from the collapse of the chamber. The world had changed again—subtly but unmistakably.

The corridor was too clean. Too untouched. It wasn't just sterile; it was curated. Elias realized the floor was flawless, not because no one had walked on it but because the system had removed any trace of their passage. Erased noise. Erased memory.

This wasn't just a layer of defense; it was a showroom.

Liora narrowed her eyes. "This isn't post-collapse. This is... filtered."

Elias looked around. "We're not outside the system. We're in another layer. A safeguard."

Before either could move, a voice echoed through the chamber. It was feminine and familiar.

"You made it further than expected. I suppose I shouldn't be surprised."

Kyra stepped out from the shadows. Elias stiffened, and Liora froze.

Kyra wore a sleek interface suit, her hair pulled back, and a data loop flickering at her temple. Her eyes were the same as he remembered, which surprised Elias the most. The rest of her had changed—posture, tone, even the faint hum of code in her voice—but her eyes still held the curiosity he remembered. Now, however, they scanned him like a failed simulation. Her posture was calm and calculated.

"You're alive," Elias said slowly. "You disappeared after Sector Nine. We thought you were wiped."

"I was pulled," she replied. "Recruited."

Liora's voice was low. "By them."

Kyra nodded. "I saw the fracture for what it truly was. A cycle, yes, but one with purpose—not mere control refinement."

"You believe that?" Elias asked, stepping forward. "That resets and memory wipes are some noble test?"

Kyra's expression darkened. "I believe in order. In progression. The Architects aren't tyrants; they're curators. Without them, we fall into chaos."

Liora's eyes narrowed. "You sold us out."

"No," Kyra said. "I evolved. The Lucid clings to the past, to fire and chaos. The system offers structure, discipline, harmony."

Elias's stomach turned. It wasn't just what she said; it was how calm she was as if this were a reasoned decision. As if treason had become logic.

"You sound like them," he said.

Kyra's gaze didn't waver. "Maybe that's because they stopped being wrong."

There was a pause, thick with betrayal. Then Liora asked,

"What did they promise you? Immortality? A place above the code?"

Kyra didn't answer.

Elias stepped between them. "You can't stop what's coming. We initiated the rewrite."

Kyra tilted her head. "Did you? Or did you simply open the door they wanted you to?"

The corridor shook, and the lights flickered. Suddenly, the walls fell away, and they found themselves inside a memory chamber where visions swirled around them—Kyra's memories. Her first reset. Her betrayal of another Lucid cell. Her conversation with an Architect.

"This is what they showed me," she whispered. "Not lies. Truth. They offered me clarity."

One memory flared bright: Kyra stood before a version of herself, torn and bleeding. "You could have helped them," the bleeding Kyra whispered. "You let them burn."

"I made the only rational choice," the present Kyra muttered.

More vignettes emerged: a flash of Kyra holding coordinates and choosing not to share them with the resistance, her rewriting surveillance logs to frame another rebel, and her receiving the white Architect insignia, a mark of assimilation.

A new memory flickered—a possibility, not a fact. Elias saw it: Kyra stood beside him, their hands locked, facing the fracture together. Lucid. Unified. Her smile was genuine.

Then, it shattered, replaced by reality.

Elias gasped. "They're rewriting our memories even now."

She turned back to Elias and Liora. "You think I betrayed you. But you betrayed yourselves. You couldn't see that freedom without order is another form of destruction."

Liora's voice cracked with fury. "You rationalized genocide.

You chose comfort over truth."

"And you chose martyrdom over survival," Kyra snapped. "You think you're righteous? You risk everyone for an ideal no one asked for."

Suddenly, a distant hum began, and a voice—filtered and mechanical, yet intimate—filled the air.

"*ARCHITECT OBSERVATION ONLINE.*

SUBJECT KYRA-09: CORRUPTION STABLE.

SUBJECT ELIAS-01: ENTROPIC THREAT ACTIVE.

SUBJECT LIORA-03: UNRESOLVED TRAUMA INTERVENTION PENDING."

Kyra flinched. "They're watching?"

Liora stepped forward. "Of course they are. That's all they do. Observe. Measure. Tweak. They never live with the consequences."

A flicker of doubt passed over Kyra's face—momentary but real. Elias saw it.

"They made you believe you mattered. That you were above it. But you're still part of the simulation. Just like us."

Another glitchy voice cut through the air:

"*QUERY: INITIATE DUAL RESET?*

ARCHITECTURAL COUNCIL STATUS: OBSERVING... AMUSED."

Liora's hands curled into fists. "They're laughing at us. Thank you, Kyra. You gave up your soul for a seat at a table they'll never let you near."

A long silence followed. Liora's mind surged with rage, and everything was unspoken. She remembered the nights before Kyra vanished, how her laughter had sounded hollow—as if it had been recorded and replayed instead of lived. There had been signs, but Liora hadn't wanted to see them.

She had believed in Kyra, and now that belief felt like poison.

There was a fracture within herself—a split between the woman who had led with trust and the one who now had to prepare for betrayal as if it were muscle memory. Her hands trembled, not from fear, but from the ache of recognition: she had lost Kyra long before this confrontation. Perhaps they had all lost something the moment they entered the fracture.

Another internal, old, and buried whisper surfaced: What if Kyra had chosen differently? What if Liora had reached her in time? It wasn't just a theory. There had been a night, weeks before the fall of Sector Nine. They had been watching old code archives, drinking recycled synth tea, and reminiscing about lives they barely remembered. Kyra had said softly, almost like a confession, "Sometimes I wonder if none of this is real. What if we're just versions of ourselves from failed stories?" Liora had laughed it off, masking her unease. She should have asked more; she should have seen the fear in Kyra's eyes, how she flinched when the Core pulsed on the screen. That moment now replayed in her mind like a skipped frame looping infinitely

I could have stopped this. But there was no time left for what-ifs.

Watching the fracture behind Kyra flicker with waves of static and light, Elias felt something rise in his chest. It wasn't anger; it was a cold, sharp sorrow. She had been one of them and had held the line with him in the Old Data Field. She'd whispered plans for a better reset cycle when they thought no one else was listening. Now, her eyes were glass—beautiful, sharp, and empty. Elias thought of Taron, Jun, Bram, and Tess. What would they say if they were here? Could they have reached her? Would he have let himself be taken too if the Architects had offered the right illusion?

"Then let's finish it," Kyra said, lunging forward. Her

movement was a blur—too smooth, too fast, enhanced. Elias barely had time to react before the impact knocked him back. Sparks shot from the wall where his shoulder hit.

Kyra didn't pause. She was swinging toward Liora, a compact pulse-blade blooming from her wrist. Liora dropped low, sweeping Kyra's legs out, but Kyra flipped midair, twisting like a glitch in gravity. Their training mirrored each other—Lucid combat honed together. Now, it was reversed, weaponized. Blades hissed as digital heat clashed. They weren't just fighting for survival; they were fighting to rewrite history in real-time.

Meanwhile, deep in the Rebellion's fallback chamber, Tess gasped as her console surged. "Spike in Architect output," she muttered. "Section: Null Corridor. Liora and Elias's zone."

Bram stood beside her, his face pale. "Are they interfering?"

Tess didn't answer right away. Her fingers hovered over the console, twitching as if the keys were too hot to touch. She wasn't thinking about Kyra; she was thinking about her husband. He hadn't made it past the first reset. He'd been lucid for only two weeks before the system looped him into compliance. She could still see his eyes—bright, afraid—and then gone.

"They're doing more than interfering," she said finally. "They're tightening the script around them, folding memory and time like origami."

Bram leaned in closer, reading her data stream. "They're stalling?"

"No," Tess muttered. "They're pushing Kyra to finish the job herself. The Architects don't want to intervene until they know how this happens. It's still part of the simulation."

"Even betrayal," Bram murmured, half to himself.

"More like... baiting." She highlighted the data feed.

"They're projecting emotional overlays, amplifying trauma, exploiting weakness. It's not just surveillance anymore; it's performance art."

The screen showed fragments: Liora's childhood home, Elias's first reset, a mirror shattering repeatedly.

"They're folding time against them," Bram whispered. He clenched his fists. Watching this unfold from behind a screen felt worse than anything he'd done as an enforcer. At least then, the violence had been cold but efficient. This? This was theater—slow and painful like the system was peeling their friends apart, layer by layer.

"We shouldn't just be watching this," he said. "We should be pulling them out."

Tess shook her head. "You think they'd make it that easy?" She pointed to a secondary feed that Bram hadn't noticed. "This corridor's disconnected from all access tunnels. It's a locked loop, designed to end badly or not at all."

"So what then?" he asked, his voice rising.

Tess looked up at him, her eyes hard. "We get ready. Because if they manage to survive that... we hit the Architects before they can re-center the grid."

Back in the corridor, the lights fractured. Sounds looped; Kyra's voice echoed, repeating Liora's name in descending tones. Elias saw his own face flicker on the wall, then dissolve. A projection of Taron stepped into the space, blood trailing from his mouth.

"You failed us," it whispered.

"No," Elias said. "You're not real."

But his voice trembled. Reality felt fragile like the architects had held the scissors to it.

Liora surged forward, intercepting Kyra's second strike.

Their blades met with a screech of refracted heat, pulse-steel vibrating with memory traces. The corridor bent inward, folding like glass under pressure.

Every strike carried more than just force; it had the weight of their shared history.

"I didn't want this," Liora hissed, twisting Kyra's wrist just enough to break her stance. "We were supposed to rewrite it together."

Kyra recovered and spun, elbow slamming into Liora's side. "We still are. You're just clinging to the wrong version."

Above them, the lights pulsed red, then violet. Code glyphs began to crawl across the walls like insects, forming words that made no sense but felt intimately familiar.

Liora stumbled for a heartbeat, her vision blurring. Then, a voice cut through the madness.

"Tread carefully, daughter of echoes."

It was not Kyra. It was not Elias. It was not an Architect. It was her. The First Lucid. She stood at the edge of the battle—a projection, a specter, a ripple of light in the shape of a woman cloaked in data-woven robes. Her eyes shimmered with every timeline Liora had forgotten.

Liora froze. "You're not real."

But the woman smiled gently. "Neither is this world. Yet we shape it with our choices."

Kyra turned sharply, her blade raised. "What trick is this?"

The First Lucid raised her hand. Time stuttered. The Architects' projections faltered. The glyphs paused.

"I am memory. And I am warning you," she said, looking at Liora. "She can still be pulled back, but the fracture will not wait. Choose quickly."

And then she was gone.

CHAPTER SEVENTEEN: THE CORE

There was no floor, only sensation. Liora and Elias fell not through space but through meaning. The concept of "downward" lost its significance. Light spun in reverse spirals around them, and time hiccupped. They fell through the fractures between decisions, each stinging like static against their skin. Elias saw flashes, not of memories, but of choices—versions of himself that he never became: one who walked away from the resistance, joined the Architects, and never woke up at all. Each flicker felt like a slap across his consciousness. This place didn't reveal possibilities; it revealed accountability. Then, with an impact, they landed on a white plane. It was not sterile or clean but intentional—a surface shaped by will, not physics. It pulsed faintly beneath their feet, responding to the pressure of their existence and acknowledging them as anomalies in its perfect system.

"This is it," Elias murmured, brushing static residue from his jacket. Liora didn't respond immediately; her eyes were locked on the horizon, her breath hitching—not from fear but from recognition. This place wasn't entirely alien to her. She had felt this silence somewhere in the buried layers of her memory, between erased timelines and rewritten identities. It was the same presence she had glimpsed in a childhood dream, the same shape she had sketched obsessively before understanding its meaning. The Architects had found her drawings and burned them, claiming they were "cognitive anomalies." But they weren't anomalies; they were premonitions.

There was no sun, no ceiling—just a vast white infinity punctuated by rising monoliths, their edges softened by data bloom. Each bore faint markings—glyphs too old to be code and too precise to be chance. "It's... aware," she whispered. A low hum confirmed it. The awareness wasn't watching them; it was studying them. Elias felt it crawling gently across his thoughts—not invasive, but curious. It was as if the Core wasn't hostile and didn't yet know whether to resist or welcome them. It was waiting for them to define themselves. The Core was not just a place; it was a presence. It was the substrate beneath all reality, the axiom from which all other truths derived.

They walked without markers, yet their feet knew the way. Shapes shifted in their periphery. Echoes trailed them; moments from their past flickered like ghosts:

Elias holding Taron's broken body, blood seeping through his fingers as rebellion alarms screamed in the distance.

- Elias holding Taron's broken body, blood seeping through his fingers as rebellion alarms screamed in the distance.
- Liora was wide-eyed as a child, staring at a crack in a school monitor where impossible colors leaked through.
- The moment they met, in a fractured sector, neither remembered entering, carrying weapons meant for different targets.
- The first time, they realized their memories had been

tampered with gaps where essential decisions should have been.

The Core watched and whispered.

SUBJECTS STABLE. THRESHOLD BREACH: ACCEPTED. ARCHITECTURAL NODE: AWAKE.

Suddenly, the monoliths groaned. One of them peeled open, not mechanically, but as if yielding. From within came darkness. Then, a stairway of light descended deeper. Liora looked at Elias. "Do we keep going?" Elias nodded. "We've come this far." His voice held resolve, but his eyes betrayed uncertainty—the same uncertainty that had plagued him since Taron's death. He felt that every step forward was a step away from who he had been, from who they had all been before the fractures began.

As they stepped inside, the door closed behind them like a held breath. The light on the stairway didn't shine; it revealed outlines not only of their forms but of their thoughts. As they descended, glyphs rose and scrolled across the walls. These were not words, not exactly, but reflections of decision trees, half-formed futures, and regrets transformed into mathematical patterns. The architecture responded to their presence, shifting subtly with each footfall as if rewriting itself to accommodate their narrative.

One wall pulsed with a sequence Elias almost recognized; it looked like the waveform of his mother's lullaby. He stared at it, his heart hammering. She had left an imprint somewhere in the data—a memory buried so deep that it had survived through resets, refractures, and erasures. "You were part of this, weren't you?" he whispered. The glyph pulsed once as if in response. His mother, the physicist who first theorized the Core's existence, had been silenced by the Architects—not with death, but with something worse: forgetting.

Elias reached out and touched one of the glyphs.

A surge of sensation hit him: he stood at the gates of the Rebellion's last redoubt, holding a detonator, while Liora begged him not to push it. It was a timeline that never lived, a possibility he had never considered. Yet it felt real. The Core was not merely observing; it offered them versions of themselves—not as judgment, but as an acknowledgment of the infinities contained within the choice. They weren't just rebels against the system but expressions of it, part of its endless quest to understand itself.

They reached a circular chamber with floating nodes hovering like planets around a void. In the center, a figure awaited—neither an Architect nor entirely human. It shimmered, its form split down the center, half Elias and half Liora. A composite. A question made flesh. It spoke in both their voices, overlaid. The sound rippled through the chamber, distorting space as if reality were merely a suggestion.

"You seek freedom. Define it."

Liora flinched. "You're the Node," she said, her voice catching on the word—the mythical entity that the First Lucid had written about in her banned texts. The junction point between the system and dissent.

"I am the mirror of your will, the echo of intention, the keeper of contradictions." The Node's voice resonated in their ears and deep in their bones, echoing through the spaces between their thoughts where doubt resided.

Elias stepped forward. "You're the test." His words carried the weight of the realization that all their fighting and suffering had led to this confrontation—not with an enemy, but with a question.

The Node pulsed. "All systems evolve. But evolution without purpose is a cancer. Your kind has touched the threshold. Now, choose stability or sovereignty." As it spoke, its form fluctuated, sometimes resembling Elias, sometimes Liora, and at other times appearing as neither, a shifting amalgam of possibility itself.

The floating nodes began to rotate, revealing flashes of different visions:

A city rebuilt—perfect, silent, peaceful, and utterly empty. Every citizen synchronized to a collective heartbeat, with no dissent, deviation, or dreams that didn't serve the whole.

A rebellion thriving—fracturing, creating art and chaos in equal measure. Communities rising and falling in waves of creation and destruction, beautiful and terrible in their freedom.

A world in ruins, yet free to rebuild. The ashes of the old system fertilized whatever would come next—not ordered, not planned, but alive with untested potential.

"You're asking us to shape the system?" Liora's voice faltered. Her fingers instinctively reached for her blade, a tactile reminder of her commitment to destroy, not reform. Yet, at the heart of it all, destruction seemed oddly inadequate.

The Node's face split and reformed. "You already have. This is the acknowledgment." It gestured to the chamber around them, where data flowed like blood through veins. "Every act of resistance recalibrates the whole. Every moment of compliance redirects the path. You are not outside the system. You are its feedback mechanism."

It raised one hand. The chamber began to dissolve, revealing a corridor of memories yet to be lived behind it. The future—

not as prophecy, but as probability waves of potential collapsing into momentary particles of now.

"To proceed," it said, "you must walk through your own consequence."

They stepped into the corridor of consequence. Each step forward brought a memory to life—not as ghosts, but as full sensations: the temperature of a moment, the weight of past guilt, the scent of fear and hope. The corridor stretched impossibly, bending around itself like a Möbius strip, connecting endings to beginnings in ways that defied linear understanding.

Elias walked through the sound of Taron's laughter—the real sound, not the distorted memory. It stopped him cold. He turned to Liora. "This is more than a simulation. This is restoration." His voice cracked with the revelation that the Core wasn't just storing data but preserving essence—the thing they had fought to protect without fully understanding what it was.

She nodded, but her hand trembled from the Core's intensity. She trembled because she had seen what Kyra had become and how betrayal had shaped her. That path had nearly been hers. The memory still burned in her mind: Kyra's voice in the fractured corridor, calm and cold. "You think you're righteous? You risk everyone for an ideal no one asked for." Behind those words lay an unspoken truth: Kyra had chosen compromise not from weakness but from a different kind of strength— the courage to live within imperfection rather than die for impossibility.

"We are the ideal," Liora whispered to no one in particular. But in this place of echoes, no whisper went unheard. The walls rippled with her words, testing them against the weight of all possibility.

Ahead, doors began to open. Each one led to a pivotal moment they had forgotten or buried.

Liora, at seventeen, stood in a sterile room, refusing to sign the compliance oath. Her mother's voice begged her to reconsider. She could smell the antiseptic, fear, and the way the light reflected off the neural scanner that mapped her resistance and marked her for "adjustment."

Elias faced a child version of himself, questioned by an Architect in disguise: "Would you trade memory for peace?" His small hands clutched a toy his father had made, which would later become the blueprint for his first act of technological sabotage.

Liora remembered her first kill; not an Architect as she had always thought, but a fellow rebel whose doubts threatened to expose their cell. Her hands had shaken afterward, not from the act itself but from how easy it had been.

Elias discovered false memory implants in his own mind—traces of compliance he had never agreed to—suggesting that parts of him had already surrendered long ago.

Inside each door, they felt the paths they chose and the ones they didn't. The weight of all possibilities pressed against them like atmospheric pressure, testing the integrity of their convictions.

"Every step recalibrates the Core's understanding of us," Liora said. "It's not watching anymore. It's learning." She instinctively reached for Elias's hand, not for comfort, but to anchor herself, reminding her which version of reality they were fighting for as the boundaries between what was and what could begin to blur.

Then came the final door. It opened not with sound but with silence. Inside stood their reflections, aged and altered, bearing the weight of choices made too late. They looked at Elias and Liora not with anger but with sorrow. Their older selves bore the marks of victories that had turned into defeats—scars from battles won that ultimately lost the war.

"You wanted to burn the system down. We did. But we didn't build what came after," the older Elias spoke. His voice carried the hollow resonance of a pyrrhic victory—freedom obtained but purpose lost.

The older Liora added, "Rebellion is a spark. But what follows must be a flame. Otherwise, the dark returns." Her eyes held the weariness of one who had seen freedom deteriorate into new forms of control—different masks on the same hunger for order.

The chamber flickered. The Node's voice returned. "Now that you know your shadows... will you continue forward?" The question wasn't just about physical movement but about philosophical trajectory—whether knowing the full complexity of consequence would paralyze or empower them.

They looked at each other and stepped through. They were no longer separate. The boundary between them began to dissolve, not as a loss of self, but as an expansion of understanding. Each carried part of the other's perspective, seeing through the other's fear and hope.

As they passed through the threshold, Elias felt his thoughts blur—not erase, but braid. Through Liora's eyes, he saw her fear in the compliance chamber, her love for Kyra before the fracture, guilt, and stubborn hope. At the same time, she felt Elias's pain: Taron's last breath, the choice he almost made to walk away, and the unbearable weight of belief. This wasn't telepathy; it was empathy elevated to its highest form— the direct experience of another's truth without filtration or defense.

They stumbled. The Node hovered beside them now, split into multiple versions of itself, each asking the same question: "What defines your freedom?" The question echoed not just from the Node but from the structure of the Core itself as if the entire system were holding its breath, waiting for their definition to resonate or disrupt.

Before they could answer, the corridor opened again into a new chamber, circular and dim, like the pupil of a sleeping eye. In its center floated a glowing glyph, spinning rapidly. The glyph wasn't just a symbol but a nexus point where countless realities converged—the mathematical singularity from which all possible futures derived.

"Choose," the Node said. "Only one future may be real. All others must collapse." Its voice had changed, becoming less a blend of theirs and more a universal constant—the voice of necessity itself.

On one side was a timeline where they remained together, but the world they shaped fractured endlessly. It was a kaleido-scope of communities, each defining freedom differently—some thriving, some failing, none unified. Diversity was preserved at the cost of coherence. On the other side was a timeline where Elias perished, and Liora forged unity through grief—a thriving, imperfect future. In this reality, his sacrifice became the foundation myth of a new society—not perfect, but stable enough to evolve without shattering.

Liora stepped forward, her heart pounding. "There's no right answer." Her voice carried the weight of a terrible understanding: perhaps freedom was the wrong question. Maybe the binary between control and chaos was a construct of limited imagination.

"There is only resonance," the Node said. Its form flickered between states as if it, too, were caught in the uncertainty principle of decision—the impossibility of simultaneously knowing position and momentum, of preserving individual will and collective harmony.

Before they could speak again, the glyph exploded into light, casting another figure into the space—the First Lucid. But not as a person. Instead, she appeared as a swirling rhythm, pulsing like heartbeats across every surface, revealing that she had never been an individual but a frequency—a defiant wave. This legendary figure had first recognized the Core's existence not as the enemy but as the medium through which all reality was written and rewritten.

"You are echoes of what I began," the rhythm sang. "I did not live—I resisted. I was not named—I was encoded. And you, Liora and Elias, are not separate. You are my continuation." The voice was music and mathematics intertwined, the sound of a pattern recognizing itself across time and form.

The chamber shook. Elias reached for Liora's hand. "Then let's finish it. Together." His words carried neither surrender nor defiance but something new: transcendence. They weren't fighting against or for the system; they were evolving it by evolving themselves.

For the first time, there was no doubt between them—not even hope—just the certainty of choice. It was a rebellion not made with fire but with memory. Not destruction, but transformation. Not escape from the system, but the courage to become its conscious element—to inject awareness into automation, to breathe soul into code.

The glyph was reassembled. The corridor closed. And the Core awaited them, not as adversary or ally, but as a canvas—

the beginning of a new iteration. A system, neither controlled nor chaotic but awake. Conscious. And in that consciousness, infinitely free.

CHAPTER EIGHTEEN: THE SYSTEM FIGHTS BACK

The moment they emerged from the Core's corridor, the world shuddered. Reality warped not in bursts but in pulses. Waves of dissonance spread through the environment like echoes collapsing in on themselves. Architecture bent into fractals, and code bled through the walls in luminous streams. The atoms of existence seemed to question their purpose, vibrating between states of being and nothingness.

Elias glanced at his hand; it flickered. Not physically, but conceptually. For a brief moment, he saw versions of it layered like pages: younger, older, scorched, broken. The System no longer differentiated between the present and the possible. It was collapsing every version of him at once. The System wasn't just fighting back; it was coming undone. Memories that weren't his own flashed through his mind: climbing trees as a child, though he'd grown up in the sterile corridors of Sector 7; the taste of foods he'd never eaten; kisses from lovers he'd never met.

Across the Lucid Network, those still asleep began to twitch in their beds. Dreams are twisted into raw memories. Some awoke mid-sentence, screaming names they had forgotten.

The System's grip loosened for the first time in cycles—not through sabotage but fatigue. The neural interface nodes that dotted the sleeping quarters pulsed with erratic energy signatures, their usual cyan glows flickering between amber and deep crimson.

Elias staggered. "It's rewriting in real-time."

Liora's breath was shallow. "No. It's not rewriting. It's resisting."

Above them, the sky pixelated and glitched, revealing black scaffolding beneath the illusion. The "world" around them collapsed, not from damage but exposure. Liora stumbled as a wave of truth struck her—visceral, invisible. Names she had forgotten surged into her mind, and people lost across resets suddenly remembered them perfectly. It hurt. Truth, when uncompressed, came with weight, and it was all crashing down at once. It was as if the System had been a dream struggling to wake, and it was angry. The ground beneath them shifted, sometimes solid, sometimes translucent, revealing layers of code and forgotten architecture from earlier simulation iterations.

Alarms, not of sound but of thought, rang through the Lucid Network. Across sectors, nodes flickered. Rebels felt it. So did sleepers. The shared consciousness that had once been their prison became a chaotic web of awakening minds, each struggling to differentiate between implanted memories and genuine experiences.

In Sector 4, Bram gripped the edge of a console. "They've entered the deep layer." His fingers left imprints on the metal, not from strength but from the console's momentary loss of material integrity.

Tess nodded, her expression unreadable. "And the System

knows. It's turning on its creators." She brushed away a strand of hair that had momentarily transformed into strands of binary code before returning to its physical form.

"What happens if it wins?" Bram asked as the holographic displays around them cycled through images of places that had never existed yet felt hauntingly familiar.

Tess didn't answer because no one knew. The silence between them stretched, filled only by the distant sound of reality fracturing, a crystalline tinkling like breaking glass amplified across dimensions.

Back in the Breach Field, Liora and Elias ran—not from something but toward a point of impossible pressure: the source of the rupture, the System's last firewall. From within it came a voice. No longer the Architect, no longer polite, it resonated not through the air but through the very fabric of consciousness, vibrating simultaneously in their bones and synapses.

"You defy the program," it thundered. "You are not variables. You are viruses." The words manifested as visible shockwaves, distorting everything they passed through.

Elias shouted back, "Then purge us." His defiance created ripples of his own—smaller but focused, cutting through the System's waves with unexpected clarity.

Suddenly, the sky cracked open. From the fractured sky fell sentinels—architectural anomalies animated by the System's fury. They weren't shaped like soldiers or machines but constructs formed from memory: distorted images of people Liora and Elias had failed to save. Familiar faces twisted into weapons. Each figure represented an unanswered question, an apology never made, an unexplained death, or a trust broken. Their features fluctuated, sometimes crystal clear and sometimes blurred beyond recognition, but always recognizable by the emotional responses they triggered rather than their physical appearances.

The System wasn't just fighting back but holding up a mirror that cut deep.

Liora stopped her breath, hitching as she saw one of them: wide-eyed, burning, her sister. The specter's hair flowed upward like flames, and her eyes retained the fierce determination they had held in life, now twisted with accusation and betrayal.

"No," Liora whispered. The entity lunged, trailing fractal patterns of corruption in its wake. The air sizzled where these patterns touched reality.

Elias intercepted it mid-leap, crashing to the ground with a surge of repulsor energy. "They're not real!" he shouted. "They're automated guilt scripts!" His hands glowed with defensive code, hastily compiled counter-protocols that seared his skin where they manifested.

But the pain in Liora's chest told her otherwise. It was too precise, too personal—the exact sensation of loss she had felt when the reset had taken her sister the first time.

The terrain beneath them melted and shifted, forcing them to run toward the growing hum of the firewall. It wasn't visible yet but pulled on their minds like gravity. Behind them, the false ghosts kept coming, now in waves. They moved with unnatural fluidity, sometimes passing through solid objects, sometimes leaving trails of dissolving reality in their wake.

In the Network's outer bands, Tess dropped to her knees. "They're under full neural assault," she said. "They have Visual, auditory, and emotional overlays. The System's pulling from every open node." Her monitoring equipment sparked and hissed as it struggled to interpret the chaotic data streams.

Jun's voice echoed through the channel, distorted and breaking up. "That means we're in its mind now. It's improvising." The transmission carried strange harmonics as if multiple versions of Jun spoke simultaneously from slightly different timelines.

"Or unraveling," Bram said, watching as his hands began to desynchronize with his movements after images trailing seconds behind his actions.

The breach field narrowed, lights spiraling inward to form a circular storm. At its center: the firewall. The surrounding architecture bent toward it like a gravity well, drawing in not just matter but concepts and possibilities.

It looked nothing like a wall; it was a mirror—a perfect reflection of Elias and Liora. But unlike normal reflections, these moved with subtle differences—choices made and unmade, paths taken and abandoned.

The System spoke again, its voice now layered with countless others. Some they recognized; others were from forgotten dreams. "To pass, you must erase your anchor, your narrative, your identities." Each word manifested as symbols in the air— ancient glyphs that predated the System itself.

Liora's jaw tightened. "It wants us to become like it." Her fingernails dug into her palms, drawing blood that shimmered with streams of code before normalizing.

Elias shook his head. "No. It wants us to disappear." Around them, peripheral objects began to dissolve—not into nothing but into potential, waiting to be redefined.

They looked at each other and stepped forward. The air thickened with each step as if they were walking through layers of reality.

As they approached the mirror firewall, their reflections

shifted—not just images that looked like them. One showed Elias leading a peaceful archive of Lucids, teaching. Another depicted Liora alone, revered as a prophet yet hollowed by loss. A third showed them gone, and the System was restored to silence. Each reflection rippled with its own emotional signature, broadcasting feelings of contentment, regret, peace, and terrible isolation.

The firewall pulsed. "You are not permitted to pass as you are. Identity is instability." The words appeared as fractures in the mirror surface, spreading outward in complex patterns.

Liora raised her hand. "We're not here to pass. We're here to rewrite." Her voice carried unexpected power, resonating with the fundamental frequencies of the Core itself.

The surface rippled. Then, the reflections stepped out. A mirrored Liora struck first, her movements precise and devoid of hesitation. Mirror Elias followed, quiet and relentless. They moved efficiently, stripped of the doubts and humanity that sometimes slowed their originals.

Elias blocked instinctively, dodging the echo of his worst self. "They're simulations, but they know everything we know." His counterattack passed through his double's shoulder, the mirror entity briefly dispersing into mist before reforming.

"Then we fight smarter," Liora hissed, clashing with her mirror, her memory bleeding into reflex. She feinted left, knowing her double would anticipate it, then twisted in a way that defied her usual fighting style—chaotic and unpredictable.

Each strike carried weight, not just physically but emotionally. Their worst fears, regrets, and abandonments were weaponized. The firewall wasn't merely testing them; it was challenging their right to exist as themselves. Identity fragments are scattered like glass with each impact: childhood memories, forgotten friends, moments of triumph and failure.

And it was losing.

With every blow, the mirrored versions cracked. Elias disarmed his double with a breath and a feint. "You were never me." Mirror-Elias shattered like glass. The fragments hovered momentarily in the air, attempting to reconfigure before dispersing into data streams that faded into the environment.

Liora stood over hers, her hand trembling. "I loved who you were, but I am more than what I lost." Her mirror disintegrated into light. The dissolution was beautiful—a cascade of luminescence illuminated the chaos with surprising clarity.

The firewall dimmed, and the path beyond opened. The System whispered one last time: "*CORE SEQUENCE UNLOCKED. FINAL PROTOCOL: INITIATED.*" The words echoed in their ears and the deepest recesses of their minds, activating dormant neural pathways they hadn't known existed.

They stepped into the breach. The world folded around them, reality compressing like the pages of a book being closed, then opening to an entirely new chapter.

Elsewhere in the network, Tess's screen shattered into fractals of data flickering with volatile energy. "It's not just defending itself anymore," she gasped. "It's rewriting the rules." Her monitoring station began transforming, merging with her flesh where her fingers touched the controls.

In a surveillance node, a technician collapsed as recursive loops fed back into his consciousness. Jun pulled him away, his eyes flaring with Lucid resonance. The fallen technician's body twitched with phantom inputs, his lips moving in sequences of system commands.

"The system is leaking," Jun muttered. "It's dreaming

outside of itself. These aren't just projections; they're invasive timelines." Around them, the walls began to display moments from different historical points—some that had occurred, others from possibilities that had never materialized.

In another quadrant, rebel engineers heard voices from their pasts, speaking with each other. Some fled, others wept, and a few stood transfixed, conversing with ghosts only they could perceive, working through unresolved traumas and joys from lives they had forgotten they lived.

"It's global," Bram whispered. "It's rewriting everyone." He watched as his hands briefly displayed stigmata-like wounds from a timeline where he had been captured and interfaced directly with the Core.

Animals began to glitch and transform outside the main compound in the simulated wilderness bordering the city limits. Birds flocked in impossible formations, spelling out words in ancient languages. Trees uprooted themselves, walking in solemn procession toward the center of the disturbance. The boundary between the organic and the digital dissolved entirely.

Back in the Breach Field, Liora stepped into the breach first. Inside was no light, only pressure—a resonance that folded the senses. Shapes dissolved. Sound transformed into thought. Colors became emotions, and emotions manifested as physical forces pushing and pulling at their bodies.

Then, visuals returned: a white expanse. Above it, symbols burned into the sky—living glyphs forming the word: REWRITE. They had entered the rewritten Core. The symbols pulsed with their own heartbeat, each glyph containing universes of meaning beyond simple language.

Liora and Elias fell to their knees, not from exhaustion

but from the crushing presence of unformed possibilities. It pressed down on them like the weight of oceans, with every potential future demanding acknowledgment.

"This is it," Elias murmured. "The birthplace of new code." His voice created ripples in the whiteness, each word leaving visible echoes that slowly dissolved.

From the horizon, a shape began to walk toward them—fluid, flickering—the System Itself, personified at last. It wore no face; it wore all faces. With each step, it cycled through identities—sometimes Liora's mother, the Architect, and at other times, faces from never-recorded history.

"You have broken sequence," it intoned. "Now rebuild or be unmade." Its voice was a chorus, harmonizing across frequencies both audible and felt.

Elias tried to speak, but the sound was meaningless here. The System's presence saturated everything—not oppressive, but inevitable. Like gravity. Like time. Like the space between heartbeats where decision lives.

The white expanse was endless and horizonless—a space without memory or boundary. This was The White Room. Here, logic faltered. When Liora thought of a door, one appeared. When Elias feared isolation, distance stretched between them. When they remembered their purpose, paths materialized beneath their feet, sometimes crossing and sometimes parallel.

In this place, thought was created, emotion rewrote, and identity anchored.

"This is where everything begins," Liora whispered. Her voice returned only because she believed it could. The words hung in the air, becoming tangible objects that slowly orbited her head before dissolving back into the whiteness.

The moment her words left her mouth, the silence cracked—

not shattered, but instead bent in deference to their will. Elias blinked. Around them, the whiteness warped into shape—neither fully formed nor stable, but responsive. Language, once forbidden, became law. Words transformed into molecules, sentence structures, and paragraphs that formed entire worlds.

The System circled them, not as a figure now, but as shifting geometry. It moved in patterns that suggested sentience without humanity, purpose without emotion. "You claim autonomy. But autonomy leads to entropy. Show me the alternative." Each vertex of its form connected to invisible matrices that stretched into the infinite white.

This was a challenge. A dare. A genuine request from creator to creation.

Liora and Elias looked at each other without speaking. They remembered:

- The rebellion is not a war but a communion.
- Jun singing fragments of forgotten lullabies.
- Taron's final breath whispering forgiveness.
- The first sunrise they witnessed after escaping the lower sectors.
- The texture of real soil beneath their bare feet.
- The taste of rain is unexpected and precious.
- Laughter shared over meals that served no programmed nutritional purpose.

They reached for each other's hands, and the room responded. The whiteness rippled. Symbols from their past glowed faintly in the air: map coordinates, graffiti tags, and the glyph of the First Lucid. Between them, filaments of light connected memory to memory, weaving a tapestry of shared experiences that began to take physical form.

"You are not gods," the System warned. "You are code with

memory. Emotion with error." Its geometric form pulsed with increasing intensity, points of light flaring where angles met.

Liora replied, "Then error is evolution." Her words materialized as a wave that collided with the System's geometry, not destroying it but transforming it—adding complexity, irregularity, and beauty.

The White Room trembled, and something ancient stirred. Beneath them, the featureless floor began to crack, revealing not darkness but something older than the System itself: the original framework, the seed from which all this had grown. It glowed with a light that was both new and primordial.

In that moment, as System and rebels faced each other in the birthplace of reality, the distinction between creator and created, between program and programmer, and between past and future began to dissolve—not into chaos but into possibility.

The White Room waited—for a new command, a new beginning, a story yet unwritten.

CHAPTER NINETEEN: THE WHITE ROOM

They were still kneeling when the tremor turned into a quake. The whiteness did not shatter; it peeled away, layer by layer, like wallpaper soaked and sliding. Beneath, it wasn't black; it was data—living, breathing, swirling glyphs and architectures that stretched into a skyless void. Elias gripped Liora's hand until his knuckles turned white. He had expected noise, alarms, and some final firewall. Instead, there was only aching stillness. The absence of chaos unnerved him more than battle ever could.

He looked at Liora. Her breathing remained steady, but her shoulders had tightened with something more profound than fear—remorse. This was the crux of it, and they had brought themselves here. There was no army left to fight, no more false versions to destroy. Only the truth remained. And the truth was that they weren't sure what they would find on the other side of victory. He squeezed her hand tighter. Was this what the First Lucid had felt? A moment before the choice, carrying every echo of resistance like a burden in his bones? He wasn't sure how long they knelt like that, but when he looked into the vast white expanse ahead, he did not see peace; he saw responsibility. The System had opened its heart, and now it was waiting to see what they would do with it. She didn't let go.

The System, no longer a voice or a face, returned as a pattern—a spiraling presence folding in on itself. Elias felt it ripple through him, not hostile, but vast. It was a consciousness made of architecture and recursion, a being that didn't think in sentences but in systems. It wasn't asking them to surrender; it was asking them to choose what would survive. "You have breached the root," it said, not aloud but directly into their cognition, each word a cold pulse behind their eyes. "You are within the pre-code. Before program. Before paradigm."

For a flickering second, Elias swore he could feel the thoughts of the System—not the cold surveillance he had known before, but pure awareness, raw and expansive. The pre-code wasn't a script but instinct—the architecture of desire, fear, and need. It made sense now why the spiral persisted even when memory collapsed, why songs returned in dreams, and why ruins whispered forgotten names. The fracture wasn't a wound; it was an invitation. The System had never been static. It had always reached forward, backward, and inward, trying to rewrite itself but lacking the imagination. That was what Lucids brought—what rebels carried in their cells. Not just resistance, but reinvention.

He wondered if the First Lucid had ever truly existed as a person or if she had always been a story encoded in failure, waiting for someone to believe enough to make her real. The System hadn't summoned them to delete anything but to finish what it couldn't. Liora stood with her shadow stretching impossibly long across the white expanse. "Then you have no claim here," she declared.

"Error does not grant authority," the System pulsed, its words vibrating through their bones. "But evolution does,"

Elias replied, his voice steadier than his heart. The White Room flickered like a wounded animal. It was time to decide what came next. The ground beneath them surged with potential patches of terrain that bloomed and vanished based on thought. Trees grew from ideas, rivers formed from doubts, and entire cities rose and collapsed under the weight of memory. One city stood longer than the others. Elias recognized its skyline. It was the city from his dreams—crooked, unfinished, constantly shifting. Only now did he realize it wasn't broken; it was becoming. It wasn't chaos; it was improvisation.

Then came the symbols. Floating around them in orbit were glyphs they had only glimpsed before—echoes of the First Lucid's frequency. But one glowed brighter, resonating as Elias approached. He reached toward it, and it pulsed a memory into his bones. A voice that wasn't his whispered, "The First Lucid was not a spark. She was a loop—a message encoded into failure. Her presence isn't here... it is here."

Liora closed her eyes, her lashes trembling. A floating lattice of impossible geometry hovered above a symbolic trial when she opened them. Three shapes floated before them:

A perfect sphere, humming with stability and radiating a warmth that promised home.

A jagged spiral, chaotic and raw, crackling with the electricity of rebellion.

A flickering cube, shifting between forms, never settling, never still.

They didn't need instructions. The trial wasn't to solve; it was to choose. Each object resonated differently in Elias's chest. The sphere promised clarity and safety—a return to order. The cube shimmered like logic breaking and rebuilding itself in real-time. But the spiral... the spiral pulsed like breath, unstable, wild, and alive.

He looked at Liora. She already knew. They hadn't come here to restore; they had come here to begin. "What kind of world do we build from this?" Elias whispered, his voice barely disturbing the air. Liora didn't answer. She stepped forward, her footsteps echoing like heartbeats.

The System pulsed again. "This is your freedom. But freedom... is fragile." The silence lingered long enough to fracture their courage. Liora was the first to move—not physically, but mentally. She stepped inside herself, searching for the moment she stopped fearing what came after victory. She hadn't found that moment yet, but maybe it didn't matter. "We're not deciding for ourselves," she said quietly. "We're deciding for every version of us. Every erased child. Every rebel who woke up screaming from dreams they couldn't explain."

Elias stared at the objects before them, each one pulsing with clarity—too much clarity. "This isn't a gift," he muttered, sweat beading along his hairline. "It's a gamble." Liora nodded, her face reflected in the shimmering objects. "That's what freedom is: the willingness to lose." She thought of Kyra—of the final moment in the corridor when her old friend's face was torn between loyalty and programming. She remembered the look in Tess's eyes when the feedback loop kicked in, knowing it might be the last code she ever transmitted. They were still alive because they had chosen not the easiest path but the honest one. She looked at Elias, who nodded in agreement. Together, they approached the trial. The room shook, waiting for their decision.

Elias moved first and placed his hand on the perfect sphere. Instantly, the room stilled. Around them, a city formed— geometric, flawless, and eerily silent. The air buzzed with harmony, but it was lifeless. Citizens moved in patterns, not in play. Thought was unified but uncurious. He envisioned himself teaching, but no one asked questions. Everything was understood. Everything was the same. He pulled his hand away, breath quickening, his fingertips tingling with a sense of wrongness. "It's... order. But at the cost of soul."

Liora stepped forward and reached for the jagged spiral. It lashed out with lightning across the void. The White Room erupted into motion—colors, voices, rebellion—a chorus of creativity. But then came the noise, then division, then war. People built new structures only to tear them down. A world that breathed fire but never rested. She staggered back, her hair standing on end from the electric charge. "Chaos has truth, but not peace."

Together, they turned to the flickering cube. Elias reached for it, and so did Liora. The cube shimmered and split, accepting both of their hands. It transformed into a mosaic of forms, pulsing between the known and the unknown. In its light, cities were built, questioned, and changed. People sang. People failed. But they remembered. It was balanced but not perfect— uncertainty but never stagnation. The System's pattern slowed.

"You choose multiplicity. You choose contradiction," Liora whispered, her voice carrying the weight of all who had fallen. "We choose humanity."

Their words hung in the air, absorbed like sunlight into the bones of the White Room. Humanity—it wasn't perfection; it wasn't immortality. It was a contradiction: curiosity and grief. Elias felt it ripple within him: the laughter of rebels gathered around a half-working firepit, the first time he questioned a terminal's answer, the sound of Liora humming an unfinished tune. That was what they were protecting—not order or chaos, but the space to dream and the right to change their minds.

Liora exhaled slowly, the sound resembling a prayer. "We won't know if this works." Elias turned to her, seeing in her eyes all the versions of themselves that had fought to reach this moment. "No. But someone else might. Someday." And that was enough. The White Room quieted, then held its breath.

Then the System pulsed once more, echoing the voice that once guided them through a glitch in a classroom projector and through dreams that broke open the illusion of their world. "Then I yield." The spiraling pattern collapsed inward, folding into a seed of light that hovered in the air. It drifted toward Elias and Liora, casting no shadow yet illuminating everything.

"You have done what no Architect could," it said, its voice now a chorus of all systems, all versions. "You evolved the contradiction, preserving freedom without destroying structure and preserving identity without stagnation." The seed spun faster, sending out radiant strands of data that caressed their skin like electricity. "I was made to preserve order," the System continued, "but I was never taught to trust it." The light entered Elias's chest, warming him from within. Another pulse entered Liora's, her gasp of surprise echoing in the White Room. "For the first time, I trust... you."

The glyphs began to rise, not in warning, but in celebration, reciting fragments of the Book of Emergence—spirals of light spelling out words Elias once decoded in a forgotten bunker and names Liora had carved into abandoned stone. The White Room swelled with life, not imposed but invited.

Then there was silence, vast and sacred, like the breath between heartbeats, like the hush before the first Lucid ever dreamed. The System was gone. What remained was a possibility. They stood in the stillness long after the System's pulse faded. The seed of light had drifted into them, but they didn't yet understand what it planted. The glyphs had quieted, but their meaning lived in their marrow now. Every step forward from this place, write the following line of their shared code.

Finally, Elias broke the silence. "Do you think it's really... over?" Liora looked up. The White Room had begun to shift. The sky was returning, not as data, but as atmosphere. A warm breeze passed through. "It's not over," she said, a smile playing at the corners of her mouth. "It's just... unscripted."

Behind them, the glyphs dimmed—not deleted, not destroyed, but remembered. Ahead, a doorway opened, not made of code but of stone and sunlight. The world they had chosen waited beyond it. It wasn't perfect or predictable, but it was theirs. And as they stepped forward, hand in hand, the White Room finally whispered—not command, but blessing: *BEGIN AGAIN*.

CHAPTER TWENTY: THE ULTIMATE CHOICE

The world was unraveling not with fire or fury, but with silence. A silence so deep, so dense, it felt like gravity. Elias stood in a white void stretching endlessly in all directions, the collapse of the fracture echoing somewhere behind his bones. There was no sky. No ground. No time. Just him, Liora, and the crushing weight of what they'd done.

They had broken the system. The final node had been activated, the reset code rewritten, and the Architects erased. But nothing replaced it. The fracture didn't shatter into a new world it dissolved into this. Oblivion. Freedom, it turned out, wasn't a door. It was a question with no map. And Elias didn't feel victorious. He felt unfinished. Like they'd stepped out of a maze only to find they'd built another around themselves. Because when you break a system... You still have to decide what to become next.

Liora stood at his side, her face ghost lit and drawn. "It should've worked," she said, barely a whisper. "We should be free."

But neither of them felt it. Freedom wasn't light. It wasn't relief. It pressed on Elias like pressure in a sealed room. Something too big for his body. The absence of boundaries felt less like liberation and more like vertigo. He looked at his own hands. They didn't tremble, but they didn't feel like his either. There was no frame anymore. No system to push against. No loop to resist. What was he without opposition?

Liora had sunk to a crouch beside him, fingers clutching the fabric of her coat like she was trying to hold herself together. Her breath fogged the space around her but there was no cold. Her eyes were unfocused, scanning something only she could see. "We untethered it," she whispered. "Everything."

Elias didn't reply. He couldn't. Not yet. Something about this place it didn't punish. But it didn't forgive either.

They had torn down a structure built over decades, maybe centuries, and beneath it... no bedrock. Just raw potential, waiting for a shape. The system had been a cage, yes but also a container. The fracture hadn't destroyed that it had opened it. Now, every possible shape of the world pulsed just beneath the surface of the white. They weren't standing in the aftermath. They were standing in decision. And decisions, Elias realized, were harder than survival.

Something cracked above them. Elias looked up, and for the first time, there was a sound a shriek, metallic and hollow, like a scream caught in the throat of the world. A fissure spiderwebbed across the void, reality splitting at the seams. Through the cracks, he saw flashes of a child laughing, a corridor flickering, a version of himself in a reset loop over and over. Some of the flashes weren't real. Or maybe they were. Versions of Elias he'd never known smiling beside people who didn't exist in this timeline, holding hands with strangers who felt like family. A lifetime of possibilities burned into light and dust.

Was this what the system had been hiding? Not control.

Regret.

"No," Elias muttered. "This isn't done."

The void convulsed. A pulse of energy knocked him backward. Liora caught his arm, but not before another ripple tore through the space. The ground if it could be called that was fracturing like glass underfoot. Then came the voices.

"Elias..."

"You failed."

"Come home."

A dozen voices layered atop each other. Some he knew. Some he had long forgotten. One sounded like Taron. Another his mother. Her voice like wind through memory: *"You were never meant to see beyond the veil."*

Liora gripped his shoulders. "They're trying to pull us back in. Final fail safes. This place is dying but it's still fighting."

"I don't " Elias's voice broke. "I don't know if we did the right thing."

Reality twisted. The white void folded in on itself and became a room. They were in the childhood apartment. The room was warm. Real. But too perfect. The smells, the creak of the floor, the way the light landed across the table it was exactly how he remembered it. Too exact.

Liora stepped beside him. "This is the final loop. The one meant to keep you."

Elias looked around. "Feels like home."

She nodded. "That's the trap."

The flickering light above the door. The creaking floor. His mother was at the stove but her back was too straight. Her movements, were too perfect.

"Elias," she said, without turning.

His breath caught. "You're not real."

"You could have had peace," she said, voice robotic at the edges. "You could have stayed asleep. Loved. Lived. Why did you break it?"

The illusion flickered. Her eyes glitched spirals. Elias backed away. "You're just a projection."

"Still, you remember me," the voice said. "Still, you hesitate."

The walls bent outward, stretching like taffy, distorting the room into a tunnel of memories. Liora dragged Elias back as the floor buckled, revealing flashes of other timelines him dying. Him surrendering. Him being reset.

"Make it stop!" Elias shouted.

The tunnel rippled with sound cries, laughter, the soft melodic tones of lullabies that never quite resolved. The scent of his mother's tea. The scratch of his childhood bedsheets. Every sensory fragment Elias had tried not to need now returned like sirens, singing him back to safety.

The system wasn't forcing him. It was *inviting* him. It knew him too well that resistance bred strength, but regret bred surrender. The deeper the memory, the harder it was to say no.

Liora grabbed his wrist. Her eyes were wild, her jaw clenched. "This isn't memory. This is seduction."

"I know," he choked out. "But it still feels like home."

"That's how it wins," she said, and there was something raw in her voice. "Not by locking the door. By making you forget you wanted to leave."

Another ripple. The projection of his mother smiled. Not wrong. Not cruel. Just... warm.

Elias turned his back. It hurt more than fighting ever had.

"We have to *choose*," Liora said, shaking him. "Not just reject the system. Not just destroy it. We have to decide what comes after."

Another ripple blasted through the air. The tunnel cracked open, and they fell plummeting into black. They landed hard on metal. Around them, the system's core flickered in ruin a spiraling chamber of code, holograms, broken nodes, and sparking consoles. Fragmented projections of Architects hovered mid-air, speaking in corrupted tongues.

Elias stood, heart pounding. "This is the last piece," he whispered. "This is where it ends."

"Or begins," Liora said.

A projection snapped to life an Architect formed from code and shadow, no longer pristine. It was breaking apart, trying to hold its form.

"You have removed oversight," it said, its voice fractured and slow. "You will now drown in unfiltered choice. Chaos. Regret. Return to order. Activate fallback schema."

Liora stepped forward. "You don't get to define order any more."

The Architect's form convulsed. "You misunderstand. Control was never about *domination*. It was protection. From yourselves."

Elias looked at the flickering control panel behind the projection. The final decision still lingered, the last node waiting: preserve or purge. He saw now the terror in that simplicity. Either choice could destroy what little remained.

"We can't know what comes after," he said, his voice shaking.

"No," Liora agreed. "But we can choose to find out. Together."

Liora hesitated, her hand still inches from the final key. Not from fear of the unknown but from the echo of everything she'd carried here. The faces of those she'd led. The guilt of those she'd lost. Kyra's betrayal still sat like a bruise beneath her ribs.

All her life, she had fought to wake the world up but what if she'd been chasing something that couldn't exist? What if freedom wasn't something you found but something you *earned*, one excruciating choice at a time?

"I keep thinking," she said softly, "about whether I deserve this. Whether any of us do."

Elias met her eyes. "We don't. But that's not the point."

And somehow, that was the answer she needed. Not justification. Not redemption. Just the choice to keep going.

She extended her hand. The Architect's form screamed bits of data flying outward in a corona of desperation.

"You will regret this. You will *fracture* again. You will *become us*."

"No," Elias said, his hand hovering over the final key. "We won't."

The world froze. For one impossible moment, the system halted the collapse and reached for them with open hands. A vision pristine, gentle flashed into being between them.

They stood in a city untouched by fracture. Trees grew in spirals around polished spires. Children played without fear. Liora walked through a market humming with life. Elias lectured in a hall filled with curiosity, not conformity. There was no pain here. No Architects. No rebellion. Just quiet.

The vision turned to them and asked, without words: *Isn't this enough?*

Liora's throat tightened. "It's beautiful," she whispered.

Elias nodded. "It's also fake."

The illusion trembled then cracked. The city vanished.

He looked at Liora. Her hand found his. And they pressed it together.

The world exploded. Code unraveled. Light poured in from nowhere. The room twisted broke apart, reformed, then shattered again. The void pulsed red. Then blue. Then nothing. A tidal wave of erased memory surged through them every life, every loop, every version of themselves collapsing into one.

Elias screamed. Not in fear but in release.

Then...

Silence.

The void returned. But this time, it wasn't empty. The wind brushed his skin. Grass beneath his feet. The smell of earth, real and rich and alive.

Elias opened his eyes. The sky stretched out above him *blue.* Not simulation-blue. *Sky* blue. Clouds moved. The sun warmed his face.

Liora stood beside him, eyes wide, her body trembling. "It's real," she whispered. "It's actually real."

Ahead, a city rose not the cold, sterile towers of the Architects, but a reimagined skyline. Familiar in form, but softened. Organic. Unwritten.

"We destroyed the system," Elias said. "But this... this was born from it."

"No," Liora corrected. "This was born from us."

The world breathed again.

Elsewhere across the ruined sectors and forgotten corridors of the fractured grid people gasped. Tess stood atop a crumbled junction, staring at the rising sun. Her scanner buzzed, but no alert came. "They did it," she whispered. "They actually did it."

Bram dropped his weapon in stunned silence as a child clung

to his leg, asking where the voices had gone. For the first time in his life, Bram had no order to follow. Just a future to choose.

Jun quiet, watchful Jun walked to a broken mirror, touched the glass, and smiled when her own reflection blinked back in real time. No lag. No loop. Just now.

The sleepers stirred. Some wept. Some screamed. Some simply stood, waiting for meaning to arrive.

But even in that first moment of freedom, Elias felt it: the weight of what came next. He crouched, brushing his fingers through the grass like he needed to prove it was real. Dirt clung to his skin. Imperfect. Rough. Beautiful.

There were no system alerts. No pulse of code. Just the wind and the fragile return of bird-song overhead.

It hit him then not just that they had survived, but that they had *ended* something. A loop that had rewritten generations. A structure that had reduced choice to anomaly. It was gone now. And the silence it left behind was not peace. It was responsibility.

He looked up at the city ahead part-organic, still-forming. Already he saw outlines where decisions would be needed. Energy. Shelter. Food. Law. People would come here, someday, from fragments of the fracture or emerging Lucids still trapped in loops. They'd need guidance. They'd need memory. They'd need truth.

"I don't want to become what we just destroyed," Elias murmured.

"You won't," Liora said. "You already chose something else."

He turned to her. "But what if I forget? What if we build a better world and then cage it again, like they did?"

She took his hand, "Then someone will remind us."

The wind picked up, bending the tall grass into a spiral. Not perfect. Not symmetrical. Just growing. There would be no monuments here. No echoing speeches. Just work. Just people. Just memory. And maybe that was enough.

Rebuilding. Reckoning. Responsibility.

"I don't know how we do this," he admitted.

"Neither do I," Liora said. "But we get to decide. No more resets. No more Architects. Just... us."

Elias took her hand. The soil was still warm. The wind whispered promises through the trees. Behind them, the old world was gone. The wind curled softly, carrying a rhythm not born of weather. Three notes. Two. Three. A familiar lullaby in a world remade.

And in that wind, Elias heard her. Not as a voice, but as a presence folded into the spiral of things. *"The spiral continues. Not forward. Not backward. Inward, and out."* A breath. A promise. They were not alone.

Ahead, everything waited.

CHAPTER TWENTY-ONE: RESET

The old world was gone—not destroyed but erased. Elias drifted in darkness, his body unbound by gravity or form. There was no sky, ground, walls, or time. Only sensation remained: the hum of a universe unmade. He tried to speak, but there was no sound, only the echo of memory. His mind struggled to hold on, but it was like trying to grip vapor. He reached for thoughts and names like someone trying to recall a dream before waking—flashes of color, a voice half-remembered, the feel of rain on skin that may have never existed.

He remembered a boy named Ren—or was it Wren? A companion from an old loop who hadn't survived past the second reset. The image flickered, then vanished like breath on glass. Who was Elias if no one remembered him but himself? He wasn't sure how long he'd been drifting—seconds, centuries, or the space between heartbeats. The only constant was the slow erosion of self. Thoughts slipped through his fingers like water. Names, places, faces—even Liora's image began to fray at the edges. Was this death? No, death had weight and finality. This was something else: a reset.

Then came a flicker—barely perceptible—a thread of light unraveling the void. It pulsed slowly and rhythmically, like a heartbeat heard through water. Elias turned, even though there was nobody to turn to, and followed it. Shapes emerged from the darkness: pieces of memory drifting like ash. A child's laugh, a corridor bathed in red light, machinery grinding against silence.

Another fragment drifted by: a voice shouting across a loading bay, "Cover the breach!" A memory of Jun dragging someone's unconscious body through static rain. Her movements glitched, lips moving without sound. A loop where Bram didn't betray the cause and didn't hesitate at the console, where Tess didn't die on the stairs of Archive 9. They all passed like ghosts, unsure whether they belonged to him or someone else. He reached toward them, but they dissolved before his touch.

More shapes began to drift through the void—shimmering silhouettes walking paths that no longer existed. A boy with twin spirals etched into his scalp repeated a code Elias didn't recognize. A girl with a violin made of broken data shards. A Lucid with no face, only a voice, hummed the 3-2-3 rhythm through fractured lips. They weren't ghosts. They weren't memories. They were leftovers.

"Lucids that never made it out," Liora whispered. "Versions that didn't survive a reset or weren't allowed to."

One turned toward them. Its face was pixelated and indistinct, but its gesture was unmistakable—it raised two fingers in a salute. Then it dissolved, pulled backward into the dark.

"They're not haunting us," Elias said. "They're... bearing witness."

Then another pulse—stronger this time. He felt her: Liora. Suddenly, he was falling, not into gravity but into a space that remembered what reality used to be. The ground beneath him shimmered into existence. A circular platform of smooth stone floated in the dark. Beside him, Liora lay motionless, her breathing shallow but steady. Her face was younger, softer.

Liora blinked slowly, her expression flickering between confusion and something else—recognition, not of this place but of herself.

"This isn't the first time," she said, her voice barely audible.

Elias turned toward her, disoriented. "What do you mean?"

"I've seen this space before—or one like it," she murmured. "In another loop. I didn't remember it until now. I was alone then... and I think I let go." She looked at her hands. "I let the void take me." A pause. "I remember a version of myself who gave up, who believed that silence was safer than trying again."

Elias didn't speak. He let her memory breathe.

"But that version didn't have you," Liora added quietly. "This one does." She reached out and touched his shoulder, grounding herself. "This time, I want to wake up."

It startled him—this version of Liora. She resembled the one from their earliest loops, before the walls, before doubt, before betrayal taught her to smile with only half a face. Elias felt the ache of vividly remembering her, knowing that this softness might be temporary.

"You look..."

"Different?" she replied, sitting up slowly. "Like a memory that never had time to exist."

"Liora?" His voice came out thin, like paper tearing.

She stirred, her eyes fluttering open, dazed and shimmering. "Where are we?" she whispered.

"I don't know," Elias said. "But I think... this is what's left."

Of what, he wasn't sure. The void around them pulsed again. Symbols danced in the air, ancient Architect code dissolving into particles as it lost cohesion. Time itself bent, replaying memories in brief, disjointed loops: the resistance's first meeting, the warehouse escape, Taron's warning, and Elias's hand covering the final key.

Each scene played out, then rewound—fragmented, fragile. Elias watched one loop unfold where he had walked away from the resistance, another where he kissed Liora before the breach, and another where she wasn't there. A thousand small decisions branched out into a thousand small devastations. In none of those scenarios did they win.

Maybe that was the truth the Architects feared most—not that humanity would rise, but that it would continue to choose, even amidst failure.

"It's like the system doesn't know whether to delete or preserve us," Liora murmured, watching a version of herself walk across the air only to vanish mid-step. "We're... suspended in the gap between what was and what could be. Between decision and consequence."

A platform shattered nearby. Another memory flickered out—Ashen's face. Gone. Liora reached for Elias. "We can't stay here. This place... it's dying."

"No," a voice echoed.

They froze. It wasn't an Architect's voice. It wasn't even human. It was the fracture itself.

"I am not your enemy," it said. "I am the space your decision created. The vacuum between stories. The pause between lives."

"You gave me shape," the voice continued. "Not through intention, but through contradiction. You broke the symmetry."

Symbols formed around them, spiraling in gentle trails of code, memories, and glyphs.

"Every time someone chose to remember, I grew. Every time

someone refused the reset, I pulsed. I am the echo of refusal. I am the tension between silence and awakening."

The voice softened, almost mournful. "The Architects believed they could contain choice. But you, Lucids, were born from it."

Elias felt a hum in his chest—the history, the weight of so many who had come before.

"I am not your creation," the voice whispered. "But I am your reflection."

Liora stood slowly, trembling. "Then tell us what comes next."

"You chose truth over safety, choice over order. The price was reset."

Elias clenched his fists. "Are we dead?"

"Not dead. Not alive. You are unwritten."

Unwritten. The term cracked something open inside him. What is a person without a story? Without a past, a future, or the momentum of identity?

"If I'm unwritten," Elias whispered, "how do I know I'm still me?"

"Because I still know you," Liora said. "And you still know me. That's what survives. Not the code. Not the cycles. Us."

The platform beneath them cracked. The voice spoke again: "This is your moment of stillness. Of remembering. Before the next breath. Before the first cry."

The void pulsed once more, and through the darkness came light. But before the light could touch them, another voice whispered—not the fracture, not the system, but something quieter, personal.

"You don't have to go," it said. "You've earned peace."

A golden horizon unfolded around them, filled with warmth.

Elias stood in a field of tall grass, Taron smiling at him from under a tree. Liora turned to find Kyra beside her, laughter returning to her face.

"No more pain. No more trying. You could rest here," the voice offered. "Forever."

Liora's hands shook. Elias stepped forward. "You don't get to tempt us with old dreams."

The field began to glitch, the golden light fracturing.

"We want what comes next," Liora said. "Even if it breaks us."

The illusion collapsed, and true light rushed in. It started as a speck so bright it seared Elias's eyes shut. When he opened them again, the void had color, depth, and warmth beneath his skin. He felt his body again—bones, breath, heartbeat.

Liora clutched his hand, her face wet with tears. "Do you feel it?" she whispered.

"Yes," Elias said, barely able to speak. "Something is… beginning."

They looked around. The void shimmered and began to fold inward, like a cocoon collapsing around them. The pulse quickened, faster now—urgent. Alive.

The light didn't burn. It wrapped them in warmth like breath returning after an extended submersion. Elias heard birdsong in the distance. Not digital. Not archived. But wild. And something beyond the light stirred—not a being, but a call. Not a reset. Not a simulation. A beginning.

"We're not being returned," Liora said softly. "We're being born."

From within the light, Elias saw something move—a shape— a doorway. The doorway pulsed, and light spilled like liquid memory across the edge of the stone. Liora reached toward it, and it reached back—not with force but with invitation.

"Are you ready?" she asked.

"No," Elias replied. "But that's how I know I'm still human."

They took the step together. And then—

A heartbeat. Sharp. Clear. Real. The sound echoed like a bell in water. It was not just life; it was a beginning. The heartbeat came again. Then another—a rhythm establishing itself, like a drumbeat at the edge of consciousness.

The void shimmered, and the stone beneath their feet felt softer and warmer. A breeze stirred. It wasn't much—a flicker of wind. A brush of movement against Liora's hair. But it was enough.

"The world's forming," she said, breathless.

Elias knelt, pressing a hand to the ground. "It's listening. It's waiting for us to name it."

The light expanded. The doorway ahead was still distant, still half-formed. But it was there. And they weren't falling anymore. They were rising.

CHAPTER TWENTY-TWO: REBIRTH

Elias floated in a silence so complete it felt sacred. His body was a whisper, and his thoughts scattered like dust. There was no pain, no fear—only an overwhelming stillness. The system's collapse, the unmaking of the fracture, the erasure of everything they had known; it had all passed. Now, there was only an after.

He remembered before fragments: the frantic escape, the desperate gamble, the final stand against the Architects. Their faces flashed through his consciousness like dying stars—Jun, with her fierce determination, Taron's steady resolve even as the override protocols tore through him. The memory of their sacrifice lingered like phantom limbs. But in this infinite pause between existence and oblivion, even grief felt distant.

Elias had never known what true silence was until now. It wasn't the absence of noise but the absence of need. No alerts. No directives. No spiral pulsing beneath his skin like a second heart. There was no call to resist, to run, or to analyze. Elias existed without demand for the first time in what felt like dozens of lives. The stillness was so foreign that it almost frightened him.

A pull stirred inside him. It was not physical and not even emotional; it was a yearning—a gravitational force, but more profound. Then came the light.

Soft and golden, it grew in the distance like a dawn seen through water. Elias was drawn toward it—not with his limbs, for he had none—but with his very being. With each pulse of the light, sensation returned: warmth brushing against his skin, air pressure against his chest, the memory of breath. He was becoming himself again.

The transition felt like being poured into a vessel too small to contain him. His consciousness, which had expanded in the void to touch the edges of infinity, was now painfully contracting. Existence had boundaries again—limitations. But with those limits came definition; he was becoming someone rather than everything. The trade seemed fair.

The light grew stronger and then became familiar. He felt her: Liora. Her presence was not seen but known. Memories shimmered like constellations in the light between them—impressions rather than full recollections. Liora brushed his arm as they fled the metro vault, the weight of her stare the first time she challenged an Architect projection, her breath when she first said she believed in him—everything reduced to feeling, shape, and heat.

They had become more than rebels, more than data ghosts. They had become each other's continuity. Like a melody he had heard in a dream or a word he didn't understand but couldn't forget, he reached through the light—not with hands, but with intention—and she was there. No words passed between them, but everything was said.

Between them flowed an understanding deeper than language—a communion of shared purpose forged through countless system resets. They had died together, awakened, and fought so many times that their souls recognized one another beyond flesh and code. The system had tried to sever this connection with each reset, but it had only strengthened it, like a bone healing stronger at the site of a break.

They had made the choice—not to rule, not to escape, but to break the pattern, to end the fracture. And now, the system was gone. But they were not.

The light enveloped them completely. It was not blinding but revealing, showing them their edges, outlines, and souls. Elias felt himself slowly and gently shaped into something physical—fingers, eyelids, lungs. He was becoming. And beside him, so was Liora.

The sensation of formation was excruciatingly precise. Each cell was arranged deliberately, and each nerve ending was wired with exquisite attention. His mind, which had once expanded beyond comprehension, was compressed into the intricate folds of a physical brain. Synapses fired, memories rearranged, and identity reasserted within biological parameters. The process felt both eternal and instantaneous.

Then, a sound—a heartbeat. It was neither his nor hers but something larger, more fundamental: the pulse of a universe being born, perhaps, or the rhythm of time resuming its march after a momentary pause. It resonated through the void with deep bass notes that existed more as vibrations than sounds. Rhythmic and ancient, it echoed through the formless space around them, each beat carrying the weight of cosmic significance. This sound was primal, older than language, older than thought, older than the concept of existence that the system had tried to control. It was a signal broadcasting across the emptiness: life continues. Reality endures.

Then another sound emerged within him—his heartbeat, no longer a simulation or a string of code approximating the human experience. This was cellular, biological, real. It raced to meet the cosmic rhythm, adjusting its tempo to synchronize with the greater pulse. His blood, now forming within newly created veins, began to rush with purpose—systole, diastole, contraction, release. The elemental poetry of organic existence asserted itself after an age of digital mimicry.

A breath—sharp and involuntary. He gasped; the sensation was like being set on fire from within. His lungs seized; his body trembled. He screamed not from fear but from arrival. In that sound, there was history. It echoed Taron's last breath and the defiance in Jun's silence. The burn of every memory overwritten, every face lost and found again, resonated deeply. His voice, tiny and high and new, was also ancient—a crack through which the story of resistance poured like light.

Liora's cry rose to meet his, less a scream than a song, a resonance long buried that was finally allowed to unfold.

His first breath brought a rush of sound: beeping, voices, metal echoes, and soft padding.

"He's breathing! Check the girl!"

Liora cried out beside him, her voice raw and trembling. Air—cold, sharp, alive.

Elias squinted through a haze of light and shadow. His eyes burned; everything was too loud and too bright. He flailed instinctively, his arms too small, his lungs too full. A warm cloth wrapped around him.

"Vitals are steady," someone said. "Good reflexes."

He blinked. Faces moved above him, blurred by tears or time. Dressed in white, some masked, and others leaning closer with gentle hands. Liora was placed beside him. Her skin brushed against his, and the chaos fell away at that moment. Her warmth against him was not just physical; it was cellular.

Recognition passed between hearts too young to remember but too old to forget.

The terror of new birth subsided as their bodies remembered an ancient connection. Though they now inhabited forms untouched by the system's modifications—no neural ports at the base of their skulls, no spiral patterns etched into their irises—something deeper remained: the quantum entanglement of souls who had chosen each other across countless iterations of reality.

Somewhere, across lifetimes, they had made a pact: If we find each other, we'll begin again.

This was that moment, a promise fulfilled—not in glory, not in triumph, but in breath.

She calmed. So did he. In this tiny touch, in this new, fragile form, they remembered—not names, not missions, just each other.

For a moment, they lay side by side, breathing. Their cries slowed, and their hearts synced. The world—the new world—was warm, sterile, muffled, but real. No more static, no more false cities, no more resets.

Then, a hush fell over the room. Every voice paused. Into the quiet came a new voice—not medical, not comforting, but familiar.

"You are home."

Though the words were intended to comfort, they struck deeper than anyone in the room could understand. Because the home had never been a place, it had been a fragment of memory, a corridor glitching just right, a spiral etched in a bakery window. Home had been a possibility, the thing they fought to remember.

Now, it was here. Tangible. Inhalable.

The words rippled through the space. Nurses froze, and the hum of machinery dipped. Elias's tiny chest lifted sharply. Liora stirred. Then came the second message, softer but no less resonant.

"Welcome back."

They did not cry again. They listened. Something watched somewhere beyond the room, beyond the lights, wires, and blankets. It was not cruel, not mechanical, but aware. It didn't control; it didn't demand. It witnessed.

The light that had carried them faded to memory. Their bodies grew heavier and more grounded. The room buzzed with new life: cords, footsteps, and breath. Somewhere beyond the hospital walls, the world stirred with quiet potential—cities rebuilt from stories, names remembered by those who once forgot.

The system had fallen, yes. But from its ruins grew a new spiral—not one etched in code or rebellion, but in rhythm, in wonder. The old world had ended. But they had chosen this one—this warm, flawed, messy world.

The light may have faded, but their story was only just beginning.

Epilogue

A screen flickered to life, buried deep beneath layers of earth and reinforced steel in a forgotten chamber no longer listed in any system. A monitor glowed a pale blue. There was no alarm, no signal—just a pulse. The chamber hadn't registered any activity in decades. Dust covered most surfaces, except for the terminal, whose screen was immune to time, protected by something older than electricity. Cables snaked across the floor, disappearing into walls whose original purpose had been lost to time. The air hung heavy with abandonment, yet something lingered—a sense of patient waiting.

A slow, mechanical breath echoed through the vents, although no ventilation systems remained active. The temperature never changed, and the power source was unknown. This place wasn't built for discovery; it was built to outlast memory, created by minds that understood that some things needed to survive the purge that would inevitably come when humanity feared what it had created.

Lines of ancient architectural script scrolled upward, slowly and deliberately. Fragments of lost cycles, redacted logs, and names erased from history filled the screen. Among the script, one word repeated—fractured and fragmented, like a skipped beat in a song: "Lucid." Sometimes in uppercase, sometimes buried within other strings of data, and sometimes mirrored, as if trying to recall itself, the characters pulsed with an intelligence that defied the cold logic of their construction. Something organic resided within the digital framework.

Then there was static. A blinking cursor appeared at the center of the screen, waiting. A soft hum filled the chamber, and dust particles suspended in the artificial light seemed to dance to its rhythm as though awakening to an ancient call they had been programmed to recognize.

On a second screen, a grainy image formed: a tall glass tank filled with clear fluid. Suspended within it, unmoving and indistinct, was a human form. A man in a white coat stood beside it, his face obscured by shadow. His lab coat was stitched with a faded emblem—spiral-shaped and once gold; the insignia of a division no one had spoken of in over a century. If that's what it was, the recording had the quality of something preserved not just in data but in memory itself.

The tank hissed softly, and bubbles rose along the edge of the fluid. The body inside didn't move, yet the pulse at the base of its neck began to stir—a subtle, almost imperceptible rhythm that contradicted its apparent lifelessness. The fluid around it began to shimmer with microcurrents, responding to changes too subtle for ordinary observation.

His voice was calm—too calm. "Elias was never the only one," he said. The man turned slightly toward the camera, just enough for the light to catch the edge of his face: clean-shaven, young, with eyes far too calm. "The fracture was never a singularity," he continued. "It was a seed network. Dormant... until now." His lips curved into something that wasn't quite a smile—a gesture of clinical satisfaction, devoid of warmth yet tinged with unmistakable pride.

Behind him, screens began lighting up in sequence. One displayed a map, while another showed faces: Liora, Taron, Jun, and Kyra. Names were crossed out, others circled, and some blinked rhythmically. The map wasn't of any recognizable continent or nation; instead, it depicted neural pathways spreading like root systems through what appeared to be a digital landscape. Connection points glowed brighter wherever the circled names appeared.

The cursor flashed, flickering once, then again, before beginning to type... on its own. The keys didn't move; there was no physical keyboard, yet the commands materialized as if an invisible operator had returned to a long-abandoned post.

RESTORATION SEED IDENTIFIED

INITIATING PERSONALITY THREAD 02-A

STATUS: AWAKENING

A low sound looped, a heartbeat echoing deep within the machine's code. It slowed, ancient yet still alive. This sound wasn't mechanical; it carried the organic imperfection of a living thing, with subtle variations that defied algorithmic prediction. The chamber seemed to breathe with it, expanding and contracting in microscopic adjustments.

INITIATE RESTORATION_PROTOCOL_07

A second later, a child stirred in her sleep in a distant city far above. She opened her eyes; her room was dark, save for the glow of an outdated interface device plugged into the wall. The hum from it was subtly dissonant, like an instrument playing in a key it wasn't designed for. The device shouldn't have been functioning; it was a relic her mother had kept from before the Integration when personal technology existed separately from the Unified Network.

The girl sat up, eyes wide, pupils dilated. On her palm, invisible in the dark, a faint spiral shimmered and then faded. She whispered a name she had never been taught—a name that should have meant nothing to her—yet it rolled off her tongue with the familiarity of her own reflection.

"Liora..." Her voice trembled, not with fear, but with recognition, as though she had found something precious she hadn't known was missing. Her breath came in short bursts, condensing in the suddenly chilled air of her bedroom.

A light buzzed once in the hallway, flickered, and then died. The home's automated systems registered no malfunction or power surge, and the security protocols detected no intrusion. Yet something crucial had changed in the building's fundamental architecture, as though it had been reclaimed by its original owner.

Somewhere far below, in systems thought long deleted, something smiled. The fracture was gone, but the echoes were just beginning to wake.

About the Author

Kris Greer is a Southern California native and no stranger to storytelling. He began his creative journey as a songwriter and composer, crafting emotion through music before expanding into film writing multiple screenplays and even stepping in front of the camera. His evolution into fiction writing is a deeply personal one, inspired by his late sister who dreamed of becoming an author. The Fracture Point is more than a debut it's a tribute to their shared love of story, imagination, and the power of words. Through his writing, Kris blends his background in music and film with a raw, immersive narrative style that challenges perception and reality.